A WORLD WITHOUT EMOTIONS
EVOLUTION

EMILIANO FORINO PROCACCI

A WORLD WITHOUT EMOTIONS
Evolution

This book is a work of fiction. Characters, names, places, organizations, facts and events mentioned are inventions of the author. Any similarity to events, place or people, living or dead, is purely coincidental.

Unstatus Luxury™
www.unstatusluxury.com

ISBN 978-0-578-30594-3

Illustrations by Cecilia Flumian

First Published in 2021

To my wife Fabiana,

for helping me edit this novel and for "seeing" where others did not see.
Together, beyond the bounds of emotions.

All the monuments and works of art that appear
in the novel are real.
Reference is made in the text to a number of historical
figures who really existed.

Table of Contents

PART ONE

The Freedom of Words

1. The Beginning of the End

Delicately, silence fills the air, slipping through it lightly, hovering over the world and everything in it, waiting only to be brushed away by the gentle rustle of a falling leaf. In much the same way, emotions seem to emulate the delicate movements of silence, although, at times, they manage to burst their way into the human soul with all the boldness of a storm. These were the final thoughts of Detective William Pattern the moment before his heart stopped beating.

Inside Happiness City's Gothic church, William's body lay inside an open coffin before the altar. The expression on his face, despite its pallor, revealed a hint of amusement. Maybe he had wanted to mock death one last time, and tease it gently with a smile. He had been dressed in a long, black leather coat lined in red satin, under which he had on a damask suit with a matching black vest, embellished with a red tie. His long, brown hair had been carefully combed and lay loose around his face; his dark eyes, once bright and full of life, now rested under closed lids.

The priest was concluding the homily for the few people present at the funeral, one of which was Beatrice, a woman with honey-brown hair and eyes the color of the sea. She had loved William more than anything, and the thought that her husband's heart would no longer beat with every passing second sent shivers up her spine. Beatrice wore a long black dress and held her young son by the hand. William had wanted a child so badly; he and Beatrice had agreed to give the child his father's name: Virgil.

A few pews back, wearing an overcoat with a faux fur collar, sat a man named Romance; his carefully groomed appearance, elegantly coiffed gray hair, and deep expression lines revealed to the world that he was a shrewd and combative person. Next to him sat Maggie, a middle-aged Irish woman, and her husband Seamus, who was also Irish; he came from a family of farmers who had emigrated to Happiness City because of the famine, managing to fulfill their lifelong dream of opening a restaurant, which they named *Martin*. Sitting in the last pew, close to the main door, sat Orpheus, a tall and thin fellow with pitch black eyes. The pews in the middle were filled with William's other friends, including Tobia, an elderly gentleman who held an ear trumpet in his lap, and Jack, a cook on a ship named *Elpis*.

The door of the church creaked open abruptly and two strange characters walked in. One of them, a muscular fellow with a patch over his left eye and a disconcerting look, known by everyone as Willy, was the captain of Elpis. The other man, whose name was Stan, had blond hair, brown eyes and a small scar on his chin, and ran a restaurant called Marleyes. The two men took their places silently in the pews so as not to disturb the funeral service.

A single ray of sunlight filtered through the large, stained-glass windows of the church, now and then caressing the fine motes of dust suspended in the air; it was as if they were trying to counteract the force of gravity with their lightness, and say their last goodbyes to William. A soprano sang Schubert's *Ave Maria*, her voice echoing powerfully through the three naves of the church, filling Its every nook and cranny.

The service was drawing to a close when, suddenly, a strange couple walked into the church: a man in a blue suit with thick gray hair, big green eyes and a mysterious looking woman. She was wearing a black suit, the same color as the briefcase she was carrying; her long black hair fell straight down to her shoulders, she was very attractive and, although her face was expressionless, her big green eyes seemed to give off a strange glow.

In that era, people in some countries around the world could no longer feel emotions and thus their faces appeared completely expressionless. If there was a person present at a sad event, such as a funeral, who could still experience emotions, they might have been able to shed a tear or two for the person who had passed away. And yet, paradoxically, the participants at the sad event nonetheless related to each other with coldness. Not one of the faces of the people present in that Gothic church that day revealed the slightest expression of sadness.

What had happened to William? Who was the man in the smart suit with silvery hair who had just walked in? What was in the briefcase of the well-dressed, mysterious-looking woman? To understand why all those people had gathered in that Gothic church on the day of William's funeral, we need to take a step back and reveal the extraordinary events that led up to that occasion, events that took place in a world where emotions seemed to be a thing of the past.

William's parents had been dead for a long time. His mother was named Madeline and his father was called Virgil. Ever since they died, William's maternal grandfather had taken care of him, raising him, and encouraging him in his studies. From a young age, William loved exploring the ruins of the "ancient" world; according to legends, human beings back then could feel emotions. When he was still a cadet at the police academy, driven by curiosity, he had gone to the city of Calicraston Ville, with the express intention of exploring an abandoned building which had once been home to a music recording studio. While he was there, he managed to start up an old movie projector and had watched a propaganda video for a strange Resistance organization called Emosemvi, whose symbol was a white mask with three red tears below the holes for the eyes. Also, inside that building, behind some padlocked doors engraved with the Minedal-e Corporation pharmaceutical company logo, he had discovered the remains of people who had once been members of the Resistance movement.

The recording studio had been abandoned long before; since emotions had disappeared from the world, people weren't interested in music any longer, no one understood its meanings or appreciated its melodies. Songs no longer filled people's hearts with joy, enrapturing them, and their musical notes no longer brought peace to people.

After graduating from the academy, William was assigned to the Happiness City Police Department. He couldn't quite understand why emotions had disappeared, but he perceived how important they were to each and every living thing. One day he met Beatrice, who lived in his building. Although he was unable to feel any emotions, he somehow felt attracted to her. This encounter made him even more curious to find out what had caused humans to be stripped of their emotions.

Not long after, William found an envelope on the landing outside his apartment. Inside was a letter written in red ink that said, "You will find the answers to your questions at Minedal-e Corporation at Disgust City 45. They have been watching you for some time. Trust no one."

Apparently, a member of the Resistance movement, whose purpose, it seemed, was to restore emotions to human beings, had just made contact with him, and was now directing him towards the truth.

After searching the internet for more information on the Minedal-e Corporation, he discovered that it was a multinational pharmaceutical company with several offices around the world. The president of MC was Dr. David Shelton Malthen, the son of the famous virologist Paul Shelton Malthen, who was responsible for discovering a vaccine for Coris-91, a virus that had reduced the world population by 35%.

In order to comprehend exactly why a pharmaceutical company had shut down the recording studio, he went to the Minedal-e Corporation headquarters in Disgust City and met with Dr. David Shelton Malthen, who told him an incredible story: members of the terrorist organization, Emosemvi, who were convinced that the vaccine meant to eradicate Coris-91 would actually kill millions of people instead of saving them, had attacked the pharmaceutical company's laboratories. The headquarters of Emosemvi were situated inside the same building as the recording studio in Calicraston Ville, and one day the police raided the building, putting an end to the Resistance organization. Everything seemed to make perfect sense. William said goodbye to the president of the pharmaceutical company and went home.

Just when the entire mystery of MC and Emosemvi seemed solved, William was contacted by a member of the Resistance group who, contrary to the claims of Dr. David Shelton Malthen, told him an entirely different story.

According to this person, Dr. Paul Shelton Malthen, colluding with a number of politicians, had developed a serum called Em 0, which would first inhibit and then slowly erase the human capacity to feel emotions. The serum was mixed with the Coris-91 vaccine and delivered through mass vaccinations; from that moment on, humans, although saved from the epidemic, lost the ability to experience emotions. Consequently, the entire population of the planet turned into quasi-automatons, passive when faced with commands from those in power.

After a number of exciting adventures, William learned that the death of his parents was actually something of a mystery, and that some members of his family had been part of Emosemvi in the past. The members of this Resistance group communicated with each other using a secret code based on facial micro-expressions, the rapid and almost imperceptible facial expressions that reveal emotions. William also learned of the existence of a serum called Reversing, which could reactivate emotions.

Although he didn't figure out if Emosemvi was really a terrorist organization or not, he had been able, after a series of extraordinary events and with a hefty dose of courage and luck, to restore emotions to many humans by making the Reversing serum accessible to all. Stan, Tobia, James, Willy, Maggie, her husband Seamus, Romance, Jack, and Orpheus all helped him accomplish this great undertaking.

With this in mind, one might wonder why the faces of the people at William's funeral in that Gothic church didn't reveal any emotion; it was as if they had been deprived of them again.

Once the ability to feel emotion had been restored to human beings, William and Beatrice moved out to the country. They wanted to stay far from the chaos of the city and raise their son, Virgil, in a healthy environment, closer to nature and farther from the concrete jungle.

Some time later, several journalists interviewed William and asked him if he might consider turning Emosemvi into a political party; he replied that the Resistance movement was created for a specific purpose and once they had achieved their goal, there was no reason to continue with the political struggle. The memory of it would surely survive, as would the close friendship that grew up among its members. By re-telling the story of Emosemvi to future generations, the memory of what had taken place in the past would be kept alive so that the same mistakes would never be made again. For this very reason, William decided to leave the police force and accept an offer to teach history at the university. Although his field of specialization was psychology, his passion for history, which had been with him since he was a child, had led him on journeys to the places of the "ancient world" and his interest never faded. He went on to specialize in ancient history, and even wrote a number of books on the customs of the Romans and medieval traditions. Because of his legendary exploits, William became something of a hero, and a great number of students enrolled in the history department just to have the honor of making his acquaintance.

With the distribution of Reversing, emotions came back to people; as if awoken from a deep sleep, they suddenly found themselves full of curiosity about a past they never knew. University students flocked to study history and department heads around the world were forced to place limits on the number of students who could enroll in each course. As a natural consequence, William became one of the most eminent and respected experts in the field.

William had no desire to make money off his accomplishments or exploit his popularity for business interests. His greatest desire was to lead a quiet life: he wanted to teach history at university and live in the peaceful countryside with his family. Unfortunately, a completely unforeseen event sent his plans up in smoke.

2. Shadows of the Past

A few years later, Romance went to see William and told him a story so absurd that it was hard to believe. Apparently, people in Europe were again losing the ability to experience emotions, and it was happening at an incredibly fast rate. Romance was deeply concerned, but his friend reassured him by reminding him that they had already won that battle: better not to listen to unfounded rumors spread by conspiracy theorists, or even worse, those who wanted to capitalize on people's fears. Romance, although not entirely convinced, said goodbye to his friend, happy to have had the chance to talk things over with him, and went back to his apartment, which was located in the heart of Contempt City.

One evening, after the sun had taken its leave for the day, allowing the stars room to light up the sky, there was a knock on the door of William's country home. He opened it and to his surprise, saw that no one was there. "It must have been the wind, he thought." But just as he was about to close the door he saw a small package laying on the ground. He brought it inside.

"Another gift from one of your admirers?" Beatrice asked in her usual teasing way.

"You're the one with all the secret admirers," he replied, with a grin.

"Not really… if you recall, you even recently received a bouquet of flowers!"

"Beatrice, those were from the old farmer lady down the road! They were zucchini flowers, you know, the edible yellow ones?"

"Right, but they were still flowers!"

William smiled and opened the package. Inside he found a videotape, the kind that people used to use in the past and which were now obsolete and off the market. Since he still owned a VCR player he inserted the tape into the slot and pressed play; he couldn't believe his eyes. The word "Emosemvi" appeared, followed by the image of a white mask with three red tears just below the eye holes. A female voice began to narrate the following story:

"Some time ago, children across the globe were given Em 0 injections at birth to eliminate their emotions. In a short period of time, wars came to an end, crime practically disappeared, and human beings were freed from hate. A new world was born out of the ashes of the previous one; people stopped suffering; there were no more tears. When all hopes for humans to recover their emotions seemed to have vanished like snowflakes in sunlight, one person, someone you know very well, founded Emosemvi with the intention of turning things around. Although the Resistance movement almost failed, it won in the end, and Reversing was distributed to everyone on earth. I truly hope that this short video has refreshed your memory. Unfortunately, after saving the planet, you made a bad decision to dissolve Emosemvi; no one else can counteract the rebirth of a great evil force."

The video then showed images of past places that were important to the Resistance movement, including the Somtlose cafeteria in Sadness City, Marleyes restaurant, and the headquarters of Rotaon Ltd, the shipping company, located in the port of Contempt City.

The voice went on in an imperious tone:

"There is now a new threat on the horizon. And you have made the mistake of hiding out in the countryside, denying the Resistance. Your duty is to protect us! The majority of people in Europe now no longer feel emotions: even children are expressionless, the playgrounds are empty."

An image of the building in Calicraston Ville that housed the recording studio and which was once the headquarters of Emosemvi, appeared on the screen.

"Don't deny your past," the narrator concluded. "Revive the Resistance and give the world hope. See you tomorrow at midnight at Gear Jesture in Anger City."

The videotape ejected itself from the VCR player. A security system built into the tape had been triggered so that no one else could ever watch it again. William was speechless. He had dissolved Emosemvi a long time ago and it was hard to believe that was now, once again, eradicating human emotion. The mysterious voice had told him to meet at Gear Jesture. He knew the place well. It was a mechanic's body shop where a Resistance meeting had taken place years ago. Unfortunately, it had ended tragically, with the killing of many comrades by MC agents. William had narrowly escaped with his life. He never expected to have to go back there.

"Are you actually going to listen to these lunatics?" Beatrice asked.

"I can't ignore a call for help! We need to figure out what's going on."

"I've risked losing you so many times – our life is perfect now, we're finally happy, and out of the spotlight. I can't let you go there!"

The two stood staring at each other in silence. Their eyes were filled with expression, all words would've been superfluous. William was willing to die to save humanity and Beatrice knew that. The ideals of the Resistance movement were alive deep in her husband's heart, covered with a thin layer of ash, that was so light that even the fluttering of a butterfly's wings would have swept it away.

"Please, William."

He sighed, continuing to stare deep into her eyes, and in that very moment Beatrice understood that she would never be able to change her husband's mind. She knew how determined he was, but she also feared for his safety. The risk of losing him was great.

"If I let you keep the old farmer woman's zucchini flowers, will you change your mind?" she said to ease the tension.

William smiled and the two embraced in the quiet of their country home. Even the wind, after blowing across the plowed fields, passing that way by chance, echoed the sighs of the young couple and sought to comfort their hearts with whispers from its gentle gusts.

That night William barely slept, except for a brief moment when sleep conceded him a little peace and wrapped him in its silent mantle. He dreamed of his maternal grandfather, Walter, who had passed away many years ago. His grandfather used to take him up in the hills above Happiness City at night to show him the constellations, teaching him as much as he could. At other times, he spoke in Latin to his grandson, who enjoyed that ancient language, even though it was difficult to learn. To help young William fall asleep at night, his grandfather told him fables in Latin, written by Phaedrus, an important writer from ancient Roman times.

His grandfather appeared to William in a dream that night: he was sitting in a wooden rocking chair and observing him in silence. In his hands he had a miniature bronze she-wolf, the hinges from a door, and a seal with a rose imprinted on it. William did not know what those objects represented and especially why his grandfather was holding them in that strange dream. Walter just looked at him, smiled, and said, "Another gift from Aesacus." Then he disappeared, as if by magic, and in the same instant, the window opened abruptly and hundreds of lily flowers poured into the room. William woke up with a start; there were no flowers around him and the window was tightly closed. His grandfather, an educated and forward-thinking person, had been dead for years, there was no way he could have helped his grandson with his project. And yet, William remembered having had a premonitory dream many years before in which his grandfather Walter had also been there.

"Who knows if this time, too, he wanted to reveal something to me," thought William, as he tried, in vain, to fall back asleep.

The next day he leafed through a book on psychology, the same text that he had studied years ago to explore even deeper concepts related to the functioning of emotions, facial micro-expressions and body language. The book had been left to him by his father, Virgil, and was full of illustrations of marble busts of Roman emperors. Although the book was about psychology and included illustrations of statues, the title was *The Cosmos and its Mysteries*. When William inherited the book some years earlier, the government didn't allow people to read texts dealing with facial expressions and body language, hence the fictitious title.

Beatrice had gone out early that morning with their son, Virgil, to a stream located at the edge of a forest not far from their home; the boy loved observing wild animals. As afternoon inched towards evening, William's restlessness seemed to increase with the passing hours. He just couldn't find peace. Even the sound of the ticking of the grandfather clock in the kitchen seemed loud, the way thunder builds up in the distant depths of a valley, breaking the silence. Beatrice and Virgil finally came home.

"Do you have to go, Daddy?" asked the little one without taking his eyes off his model ship.

"Yes, but I'll only be gone a short time. Just a few hours."

"You always say that, but when you go to the university you always disappear for such a long time. When you come back, can you bring me a present?"

"What would you like?"

"A toy camera."

"And here I was thinking you wanted a cradle for your doll," William replied teasingly.

"Daddy, you know how much I like cameras! Really! I'm not kidding!"

Just then, Beatrice rushed into the room and gestured for William to follow her. The two went into their bedroom. She quickly closed the door behind her and waved a piece of paper in front of him.

"Do you know what this is?" she asked, having a hard time holding back her anger. "I found it in the mailbox. It's an anonymous message saying you shouldn't go to Gear Jesture tonight."

William took the piece of paper, on which a short message had been written in red fountain pen ink. The lettering was elegant and looked like the work of a calligrapher. "Stay home tonight. Prepare for the worst."

"We can't live without you… We've earned our peace and quiet, haven't we? Let others fight this battle!" Beatrice cried.

"Listen, every human being is born for a specific purpose. I was born to follow my star. My destiny is already written for me and for some mysterious reason I can't back out."

"We always have a choice! This is the possibility that gives us freedom. Please, do it for Virgil. Think what your father would have done if he were in your shoes."

"That's exactly why I'm doing it! I'd like to give our son a better future, a world where people are free to hug each other and do what they please. I will never let anyone give him an injection that will make his face lose all expression. If my father were still alive, he'd tell me to follow my destiny, and that's exactly what I will do."

Beatrice stormed out of the room. William made his way over to the nightstand. After moving it slightly to one side, he raised a wooden slat in the floor and pulled out a small pistol that he secured to his ankle with a holster. An old academy friend named Leonardo had suggested he carry a second pistol in case of emergency. A shadow came over William's face when the memory of his former comrade came to mind. Leonardo had once said: 'What will happen if, one day, human beings feel emotions again and they start fighting? Better be prepared. Don't risk it. Do what you have to do to stay alive. As soon as I finish the academy, I'm going to go buy an extra gun and I'm going to name it Second Chance.'

Suddenly, a number of memories came back to him. But right there and then he had to keep them under control and not risk losing his lucid state of mind. The best thing would be to keep them concealed under a blanket of time that protected like a cautious guardian, and keep them at bay.

He took off his work clothes and dressed in a damask suit and his long black leather coat lined in red satin. Then he secured another gun to his belt and prepared to leave. He left the house without saying goodbye to Virgil and Beatrice, knowing that a farewell would bring him too much pain. He was aware he was taking a risk, but Emosemvi needed him and he was willing to fight like a mythological hero to ensure that human beings could enjoy their freedom.

He went to the barn, whipped off the cloth that protected his iridescent colored motorcycle, causing a cloud of dust to fly up and fill the air, making it almost impossible to breathe. The first rumble of the engine stirred up the straw in the barn; the motorcycle, as if it had been waiting for that moment for a long time, emitted a deep rumble and off he roared.

3. An Unexpected Encounter

William arrived in Anger City early. As he glanced around the public park, he remembered how, years earlier, he had met with a kid who was affiliated with the Resistance there, and how that kid had given him valuable information.

Gear Jesture was closed. All the city streets seemed to be submerged in a strange, deep silence. He got off his bike and knocked four times on the roller shutter of the body shop, waiting. The seconds passed. He was tense. Even though there wasn't a soul around, the risk of an attack was high. The humidity of the night air began to take over the world around him, wrapping it in its embrace, and a strange fog fell over Anger City. Time passed, there seemed to be no trace of William's contact.

"Was he intercepted or killed?" he wondered, looking around suspiciously.

A creaking sound from inside Gear Jesture made him jump, so he reached for his gun and prepared to fire. The shutter snapped open. Not even the light from the street lamps could illuminate the dense darkness of the place. A mysterious, deep feminine voice invited him to enter from within the shop.

"First, tell me who you are, then I'll decide whether or not to come in. What do you want from me?" William asked.

"It would be better to ask who you have become and how much country life has stifled your love for Emosemvi," the mysterious figure replied from within. The voice sounded quite familiar to William. A thought came to him, and he matched the voice with the face of a person who had died long ago.

"No, it can't be," he said to himself, dismissing his absurd thought. It was just too bizarre to even consider.

"You have grown weak, my son. I hope you aren't angry that I raised the Resistance from the ashes."

From the darkness of Gear Jesture a woman came forward; the light of the street lamps seemed to increase in intensity, as if even those inanimate objects wanted to take part in what was happening.

"Mother!" exclaimed William.

Madeline stood before him in an elegant dress, her white hair gathered on her head. It couldn't be true: she had died years ago. As crazy as it might have been, William thought for a moment that he was looking at a ghost. Then, trying to gather the last crumbs of rationality, he concluded that it was a hallucination due to lack of sleep. He blinked a few times but his mother did not disappear the way a dream would with the first light of dawn. Rather, she stepped forward and embraced him tightly. William felt a twinge in his shoulder and left leg, in the places where he had been shot some years before. The world around them stopped; the fog seemed to clear as if to frame this special moment: a mother who had been cruel to her son in the past was trying to make up for her mistakes. William couldn't believe his eyes and, even more, he wasn't sure he could fully trust her.

The two entered the body shop. The strong smell of motor oil hung in the air. Inside, sitting in a semicircle on colored, folding metal chairs, were the heroes of the Resistance who had contributed through heroic deeds to restore emotions to human beings. Romance was there, wearing the same brown coat with its fur-lined collar as he always had. Sitting next to him was Stan, the well-known owner of Marleyes restaurant, and old Tobia, who raised his antique horn-shaped ear trumpet in greeting. James, the homeless man, stood across from him, reading a magazine. Meanwhile, Maggie, Romance's secretary, and her husband Seamus, were talking to Willy next to a car that had its hood propped open. As soon as Jack and Orpheus saw William they made their way over to him, but Madeline raised her hand to stop them. She needed to talk to her son first and explain what was happening.

"Mother, I saw you die," he said. He had a hard time speaking because of the shock he felt at seeing her. He remembered how she had taken her last breath years earlier, sprawled on a cold floor in an underground room, lit up by a flickering neon light.

"At the time you were injured, but you didn't die," she said in reply. "Well, I didn't die either. I was still conscious when help arrived. I asked them to treat you first and take you by helicopter to the hospital. Before I lost consciousness I ordered my men to tell your friend, Orpheus, that I had died. If emotions would ever return to the world, I would need cover, otherwise they would have hunted me down. By the time I healed from my wounds, the world had changed. The Reversing serum had been distributed; if I had come out into the open I would have certainly been killed. While you were leading your life in the countryside the world changed again and now danger looms over us. It was I who had one of my men send the videotape to you, I'm the one who called this meeting of the members of the Resistance."

Madeline sighed as if trying to relieve herself of a burden and then went on in a firm tone of voice. "I have watched my grandson Virgil grow over the years from afar. I suggest you keep a close eye on him as he is developing the same stubborn character that your father had. You have built a beautiful family and for this I am happy. Unfortunately, neither your father nor I were able to give you such a family. I did not contact you sooner, my son, because we have been fighting for two warring factions. This is our fate, and there is nothing we can do to escape it."

William felt mixed emotions run through him. On the one hand, he instinctively craved the attention of a mother he had never had, but on the other hand he couldn't forget that she had almost killed him in the past.

"Mother, I'm finding it hard to believe anything that you say. I've been betrayed too many times. I survived the pain of losing you by letting time take its course. After all we've been through, I don't think you can expect your son to throw his arms around your neck and hug you."

"Certainly not! We'll have a chance to catch up later. Now let's go talk to the others."

They agreed to make time to be alone and talk. They had many things to clear up and the wounds from what had happened in the past were still raw. Although Madeline wanted to be as firm as ever, she felt her heart soften with her son's presence.

The two stepped forward. The others came up and embraced their leader. They looked at him with the same admiration they had shown him in the past; with courage and cunning he had led them to victory, freeing the world from the dominance of the Minedal-e Corporation.

Madeline was the first to take the floor. Solemnly, she said, "In the past I made many mistakes. I thought the best thing was to deprive human beings of emotions, to extinguish all forms of cruelty in them and to end wars. I asked myself why a person should cry at a funeral for the death of a loved one and have to experience the emotion of sadness. I found it pointless, unnecessary. But then, thanks to William, I re-considered the work of my ex-husband, Virgil. Although he had a difficult character, he was right about everything: every living being has the right to choose whether to do good or evil."

Everyone there listened to Madeline's speech attentively, feeling the weight of her austere gaze and her determination. Just like her son, with her words and her tone of voice, she was able to reach people's hearts.

"About a month ago, I contacted Stan and asked him to summon the members of the Resistance, and I even met with some of them several times. Now a new threat looms over the world. A mysterious man has, in a short period of time, eliminated all emotions from the people of Europe and will soon be able to conquer all the countries of the world, if he isn't stopped. This is the same individual who ordered Happiness City District Chief Richard McMillan to fire on protesters during clashes at police headquarters. Fortunately, the officers on that occasion did not open fire on the crowd because, although they felt no emotion, they were not killers; they would never fire at unarmed people. The world changed that day, but evil was not completely eradicated. The man with the mysterious identity has regrouped and is vigorously launching a counter-offensive."

Looking intently at her son she went on. "By retreating to the countryside, you have shut out Emosemvi. The world needs you. If you refuse to take on the challenge, my grandson will not have a future."

Waving his ear trumpet in the air to be noticed so he could take the floor, old Tobia intervened. "We met in this very body shop years ago when I asked William to lead the Resistance and defeat the evil forces that threatened the earth at that time. Well, here I am again today repeating my request. Without your charisma, ingenuity and cunning we have no chance of defeating this new threat. It's on the horizon, about to descend upon us. Guide us as you once did and we will follow you all the way to hell if need be!"

A deep silence fell over the room, settling around them as if someone had shaken out a dusty old blanket and the dust, like silence, settled over them. All eyes were on William.

"Thank you. What can I say? You are all heroes. Together we fought and won, emotions were returned to humans and the world found its balance." Shaking his head, William continued, "This morning I was determined to fight to bring freedom to the world again, but now, especially after seeing my mother, I have changed my mind. Everything has a beginning and an end. It's time to pass the baton." With the subdued tone of someone who has been defeated after losing a battle, whose outcome cannot be changed, William concluded: "I need some time with my mother to understand and clarify what happened in the past. I want a normal family and a quiet life. I'm not backing down, but I'd rather stand on the sidelines and observe and then eventually decide how to act."

"Unfortunately, it's too late for that," Maggie said, "Emotions are vanishing around the world as we speak, and strangely enough the media isn't talking about it."

"Is it possible that in this day and age a news story like this isn't covered by the media?" Romance asked, getting to his feet in a huff, as if unable to contain his anger.

Stan, who came across as more rational, answered in a composed manner. "Let's try and keep our heads and understand what is going on. Maggie's right. It seems to be an irreversible process. There's an explanation for the way the media is behaving. As neither the journalists or staff members of all the various editorial offices have any emotion, even the will to spread the news has disappeared. Let me be clear: if I were a journalist I would try to tell people about an important fact that concerns them directly. However, if that fact left me completely indifferent, how could it possibly attract my attention? What doesn't generate an emotion, however small, is simply ignored."

Tobia raised his ear trumpet again. "We needed you in the past and we need you now! Follow your destiny!"

William was silent for a moment, then stood up. He spoke quietly. "I can't do it this time. Emosemvi has had its moment of glory, we did what we set out to do, but now it's a relic of the past. Let's allow international security forces to deal with this case. I hope you understand my desire to keep little Virgil out of all of this."

Up until then, Jack had been silent, looking pensive and stroking his thick black beard. Then suddenly he exclaimed, "There will be no future for your son if we don't act now!"

Just then, Madeline's phone rang. As she took the call, her face grew dark. "I understand. We'll be right there. Hide them and keep them safe!" She turned to William. "Beatrice and Virgil are in danger, we have to go."

William rushed out of Gear Jesture with Madeline. They got on the motorcycle and sped off towards the country house. On the way, Madeline explained that she had left one of her agents, one of the few who were still loyal to her, in front of Beatrice's house to watch over William's family. The phone call she received at Gear Jesture came from that agent. He had called her to warn her that something terrible was about to happen, but the conversation was cut short.

Once they arrived at their destination, William saw that the front door of the house was ajar. He pulled out his gun and kicked it open.

"Beatrice!" he shouted, quickly surrendering all hope of hearing her voice to the silence that reigned in the house. A cyclone seemed to have struck inside. Obvious signs of a scuffle were visible everywhere. William entered the kitchen, followed by his mother. Lying on the floor in an unconscious state and with a gunshot wound to the abdomen was the agent.

Madeline approached him. "Joe, what happened? I'm calling an ambulance!"

The agent regained consciousness. "I tried to protect them..." he said softly, his eyes closing as he took his last breath.

On the kitchen table was a piece of paper with a message on it, written in pen.

"They kidnapped your son and your wife. We wanted to protect them, but we came too late. There's little time left. Emotions are leaving all human beings. Soon the world will change again. If you want to see your family again, go to Italy. Go to Rome and get a room in Bona Fide Hotel near Piazza della Rotonda. We will contact you. Destiny always finds its way."

William slumped to the ground as if he had been drained of all his strength. Madeline read the message. Finally showing some sensitivity, she brought a hand to her heart. "What are we going to do now, Will?"

"I don't have much choice. We have to act now. Contact our comrades at Gear Jesture and tell them to stand by. MC has dragged us into this and they will regret it! Tonight, Emosemvi is reborn!"

Madeline left the house and made a phone call to her companions, telling them not to move from the body shop, while William went to the bedroom and pulled out a necklace from a drawer with a heart-shaped pendant and the letter "W" engraved on it. He had given it to Beatrice a long time ago and it symbolized all of their love. He clutched it to his heart and put it around his neck, then got into his car and drove back to Gear Jesture with his mother. As soon as he walked in, his friends came up to him.

"What happened?" asked Willy, visibly concerned.

"They've kidnapped Virgil and Beatrice. Most likely they're being held captive in Europe," William replied. With more emphasis and the tone fitting a true leader ready to lead an army, he exclaimed: "Tonight the voice of Emosemvi will be heard again! We will make our enemies tremble! We will, once again, restore order to the world!"

Shouts of jubilation filled the air. Emosemvi was officially back in operation and ready for action! William would lead the Resistance to victory again, even though it felt like such a thing was as distant as a star in the sky; the path to get there would be uncertain and full of pitfalls.

"Romance, we need your help. We can't take a plane to Europe because it would be too dangerous. In all likelihood, they're already spying on us and our enemies might kill us on the way. If we traveled by ship, not only would it be safer, but we could avoid custom inspections and take all kinds of equipment with us. Can we count on you?"

"Yes, of course. Use the Elpis. She's docked at the port of Contempt City at Pier 18. In fact, I can also make the Elpis II, which is moored at Pier 23, available to you. You know, since emotions have returned among humans, there's been more work, so I bought another ship, one that's identical to the Elpis. I even had her painted in the same colors."

"Thank you for your help, Romance. Keep the Elpis II in the harbor. We will sail in two days, at first light, on the Elpis. Tobia, James, Maggie and Seamus: stay at Gear

Jesture and set up an operations center to give us logistical support. We will stay in contact with you and call if necessary. Make sure to get an internet connection, a shortwave radio and other equipment, I'll get you a list. Forgive me for not telling you now, but we have been betrayed many times and our operational protocol for maintaining the secrecy of our operations is now in effect. Only I will know the individual tasks assigned to each of you. Romance, Stan, Jack, Orpheus, and, of course, Captain Willy, will all come with me."

"I think there's a name missing from your roll call," Madeline said.

"Mom, I can't risk losing you again. I'm sorry we didn't have time to talk. We still have a lot to sort out. But I'd rather you stay safe."

"You're going to need my help and expertise. I'm not going to stand by and watch you risk your life! I also think that the plan should be changed because there are still lots of details to be worked out."

After briefly mulling it over, he replied with some hesitation. "Fine, Mother, you can come with me. You've been in a position of leadership your whole life but now I make the rules. And my plan won't change one single iota."

Madeline turned her face to the wall in annoyance. She couldn't stand being told what to do, especially since she had accumulated a great deal of organizational experience over the years. But at the same time, she understood that she had to accept the rules set by her son if she wanted to regain his affection.

The two days passed quickly. The moment of departure arrived. William felt sad: he never thought he would find himself in the position of having to save his wife's life again. She had already been kidnapped in the past and fortunately he had managed to free her, but now his son was involved. Everything was so complicated. He had always dreamed of having a family. Now, just when happiness had arrived, he found himself in danger of losing it. And he felt guilty for not being able to protect Beatrice.

4. Fascinating Journey

As William and Madeline were driving to the port, they got the feeling they didn't know each other well. They both had a lot to say but didn't know where to start. Usually strong and assertive, in that moment, William had a hard time dealing with his emotions, as if anger and love had done battle within and left him feeling stuck.

His mother felt the same way. She didn't know how to break the silence either. She loved her son and, although she watched him grow from a distance over the years, when he had put MC's existence at risk with his investigations, she had reluctantly made the decision to have him killed. It was a rather unusual choice for a mother, but at that time Madeline thought she was acting for the good of humanity. In addition to being a brilliant scientist, she was also very ambitious, which had led her to be fascinated by power and to want to move forward with her career within MC at any cost. After proving herself to be more astute than any of her other colleagues vying to reach a prominent position within the organization, she dedicated herself to the only work she considered important. She didn't mind holding the destiny of humanity in her hands: she had learned to manage all kinds of situations with cool rationality, showing that she had the makings of a true leader.

As the silence in the car became heavier and heavier, they grew closer to the cemetery of Contempt City. "So many memories," William thought. There was where he had previously met a former police colleague who had unfortunately been murdered by MC.

"You look pensive," Madeline said warmly.

"When I pass by a place like this, I start thinking about the past and many painful experiences come back to me."

Madeline didn't know her son well and tried to console him, but unfortunately she chose the wrong words. It was as if she couldn't fully understand his feelings.

"The past is the past and it must be forgotten," she said.

Like a river raging up and over the banks, William lost his patience. "The present is the result of our past! How can you not understand that?"

His mother had spent her entire life running a large organization, coldly calculating every little move, and over time her soul had hardened. She couldn't find the right words to answer her son. Sometimes, however, maternal instinct can break down even the most solid wall built with bricks of rationality. Madeline collapsed into tears. Sobbing, she said, "I'm sorry, my son! I'm sorry for everything. I can't find the right words now, but I want to make up for it. Give me a chance to be near you. I want to see my grandson grow up. Let's make time to be together, we can clear everything up. I'm really sorry! Please don't shut the door in my face!"

William sighed deeply. He was still very conflicted but seeing his mother break down like that had touched him deeply. However, at that moment he could only say, "Fine. We'll find time to talk."

Madeline continued to sob until they reached the port. Strangely enough, it was deserted. There wasn't even one security guard at the entrance. They parked the car right in front of the Rotaon Ltd building, which had been reduced to ashes by men from MC and then rebuilt with even better materials. As soon as he got out of the car, William walked towards the pier with his mother. After drying her tears, she had gone back to being a woman in charge and assumed her usual icy expression. The large ship on which they would embark was moored at pier 18. Painted on the side of the ship was an earthenware vase with the name "Elpis" written across it. Their companions were waiting for their leader on the main deck, lined up like soldiers ready for inspection.

"I think we can do away with all formalities," William announced as soon as he saw them. "I know what each of you are worth, there's no need to line up for me. The captain of this ship is Willy and all of us aboard must listen to him. Let's get ready to sail; time is not on our side."

Willy adjusted the patch over his left eye, feeling flattered by the words spoken by his leader, ready to follow him across the sea.

"Gentlemen," the captain announced, "It will be a long journey, so polish your weapons and be ready for the worst. I will do anything I have to get you safely to your destination, even if it means losing my other good eye." Then, turning to William, he said, "Allow me to introduce you to some of the crew."

Lined up in front of a lifeboat were a few of the crew members. There were some bizarre characters: an eagle-eyed sailor named Mikey, who always had his inhaler in his hand because he suffered from asthma; Clark, a tall and hefty man with short hair and an unruly quaff, who was a Spanish-speaking bomb disposal expert. Then there were two brothers who worked in the engine room, jokingly called "the gentlemen" by everyone because even though their clothes were stained with engine grease, they were always well-combed and their beards were always carefully groomed; their names were Karl and Jacob and in their free time they loved to entertain the crew with fantastic stories about adventurous buccaneers.

"Allow me to introduce you to Lieutenant Commander Marko," Willy said, indicating a slim, toned man in an immaculate but frayed white uniform. He looked like an easy-going person but had peculiar eyes: icy blue in color, with veins similar to small stalactites.

"A pleasure to make your acquaintance. Captain Willy has told me a lot about you," said Marko, visibly excited to meet William, who was considered a living legend.

"My pleasure, Marko. Have you been working with Willy for a long time?"

"About two years, sir."

"Interesting. Why are you lying?"

"I don't understand. What's that?"

"When you replied, you took a step back. In body language that's called a gestural retreat. It means you find the question uncomfortable and in all likelihood you lied."

"I don't know what you're talking about."

"Good. Now you're also showing anger. You briefly clenched your fists. You know, peripheral vision is good for noticing details that many people miss. Plus, a micro-expression of anger appeared for less than a second on your face. Remove your mask!"

At that point Willy intervened. "Marko, I forgot to explain something. William can read body language and facial micro-expressions." Then, turning to William with the repentant tone of someone who has committed a sin and wants to confess, he added, "It's true, he lied, but not because he is our enemy. His intentions are good. My crew is used to being very discreet. Unfortunately, in the past, the Minedal-e Corporation agents used to breathe down our necks. Each of us has learned never to reveal details about our service on this ship or about our private lives. However, I want you to know that I trust him a great deal."

"I understand. Not a problem," William replied.

"Allow me to introduce you to three other members of the crew." The captain called forward two men dressed in mechanic's overalls and a woman wearing a clean, perfectly pressed white uniform. One of the two men had a black crew-cut and green eyes with blue speckled irises. The other man was of sturdy build, wore a sailor's cap pulled down to the tips of his ears and had a bristly gray beard that made him look wise. If he hadn't been wearing his work clothes, he would've looked like an officer or even the captain of the ship. The woman was strikingly beautiful. She had elegant features and a well-shaped, generous mouth. Her large green eyes were the mirror of a fascinating and deep soul. She looked down on the world as if she was aware of her extraordinary beauty, like a queen.

Pointing to the man with the black crew-cut and eyes of a strange color, Willy said, "This is Ephialtes. He works in the galley. His companion is Bill and he takes care of the ship's maintenance. And this is Medea, Ephialtes' sister and expert cartographer in charge of charting the routes. There's another woman aboard: Acli, the ship's medic."

William saluted them in greeting, which was followed by a moment of awkward silence. The captain of the ship spoke up.

"William has this effect on people. They prefer to remain silent rather than risk contradicting themselves with their body language. Don't worry, team, William is fair and he won't ask questions about your true identity."

Medea showed that she was more resourceful than her companions and took the floor. "It's an honor to meet someone who has saved the world. I imagined you to be taller and more muscular - but that's okay."

"Yes, it's true. Comic book heroes are all tall and muscular but, in reality, the world is saved by people who know how to use their brains, regardless of their size."

Medea looked like a woman with a strong character; it was hard to resist the charm of her magnetic gaze. She always commanded deep respect, and yet no one knew exactly why she had boarded the ship.

"You strike me as a determined woman," William stated.

"To survive on a ship full of men you have to have character. The last sailor who tried to bother me was fished out of the water two days later."

"Well, determination does help in life. How did you meet Willy?"

The woman, however, chose not to reply and instead looked out to the horizon.

Willy interjected, "As I told you before, it's going to be hard to find people here willing to answer questions. I'm sorry I can't introduce you to everyone; there are many others who are now busy with their duties. Anyway, now follow me, and I'll show you to your cabin. Are you sure you don't want to sleep in the hold like last time?"

"This time a comfortable bed will be fine, thank you," William replied wryly, winking at the ship's captain.

The Elpis put out to sea as the sun beamed down on her with its warm rays. A single cloud seemed to follow the ship as if it wanted to catch up to it, until it vanished, taken with the wind.

William and Madeline met up on the main deck. Actually, she had been waiting for him for hours. She wanted to talk to him and had prepared a good speech. She wasn't sure if it would help her relationship with her son, but she wanted to try, even though she was aware that she didn't just have to mend the relationship, she had to build it up from scratch.

"Have you eaten, William?"

"Not yet, I'm curious to see what Jack's been cooking."

"Look, I was being bluntly honest in the car: I do fine when I have to plan something, but with feelings I'm a mess. I may never be able to make it up to you, and in fact, I don't see how you could feel even an ounce of love for me, but I am ready to love you unconditionally, even though I know I don't deserve a shred of attention from you."

"I appreciate your words, but it kind of sounds like a movie script," William said, shaking his head, while also hinting at a smile.

"It's true, I prepared a speech for you. I'm used to planning everything, but I know that I'm not dealing with a colleague, I'm dealing with my son. So, let's do something, let's start over and forget what I just told you. Let me try and speak from the heart."

Tears poured down her face, which were swept away by the wind and into the salty ocean. "When everything is over and we have brought Beatrice and Virgil home, I could rent an apartment nearby. I don't want to disturb your privacy, mind you, but I'd like to be able to see you now and then. Even just two minutes a day, if possible. I'd also like to play with Virgil and read him stories, and tuck him into bed. Maybe I'm asking too much, but I'm speaking with my heart in my hand. I've made mistakes in the past, I know I have to pay for them, and if you don't want to have me nearby I will understand."

At first, William shook his head, but then nodded. "For years I've had to work through the guilty feelings of shooting you. Sure, I did it to defend myself, but the thought of killing my mother has haunted me for a long time. Even so, I'm willing to let time heal things."

Madeline hugged her son tightly and, with a heart full of hope, she returned to her cabin.

The ship sailed on for many hours. When the sun was about to go to sleep, lulled by the splashing waves and the reflection of light on the golden foam, William made his way to the mess hall.

At one table, Medea and Madeline were talking. In a corner, Ephialtes and Bill were finishing their meal in silence. Jack, the ship's cook, had prepared an excellent pasta dish with shrimp and cherry tomatoes; the crew had been attracted to the smell of the food like bees to flowers. William, being of Italian descent, loved pasta, especially when cooked by his friend, Jack. He ate his portion, but then he noticed something strange on the bottom of the plate. At first he didn't know what it was, then as he wiped it clean with some bread, he realized that a message had been scratched into the metal plate: *There's a spy on board, watch your back*, it said. Just below was a Latin inscription: *Beati monoculi in terra caecorum XXI - IV*. The words didn't seem to make sense. And what's more, William didn't think that anyone on Elpis, other than himself, understood Latin. He put his hand on his gun and looked around, but none of the people in the cafeteria seemed to take notice of him, except for Medea who left Madeline and came over to his table. She had changed out of her uniform and into a green Rotaon Ltd jumpsuit, and although this item of clothing had nothing of an evening gown about it, it revealed the curves of her body.

In a gracious, sultry manner, she said, "I like having a strong and intelligent man around; there aren't many of them on board."

William didn't feel attracted to her, but her beguiling gaze made him uncomfortable. The woman's big green eyes were trying to corrupt his willpower.

"Thank you, I'm just trying to do my duty. Fate is always forcing me to face situations from which I would like to get away. The more I try to live in peace, the more I get sucked into a vortex that is impossible to avoid." He paused a second and then continued. "How long have you been working for Romance?"

"Why should I answer you now? I didn't do it before and I don't want to talk about it," she said, visibly annoyed.

"No need to answer. Let's see: you've been working for him for a year." William kept his gaze fixed on Medea's face, while with peripheral vision he watched the rest of her body for telltale signs. "No, wait, you've been working for him for two years... or maybe even three." The woman crossed her legs and turned her gaze toward the kitchen, rolling up the sleeves of her jumpsuit. On her right forearm was a tattoo depicting a dragon, and on her left two small scars.

"Did you choose to board the ship of your own free will?" William pressed her.

"When will you get tired of asking me questions? I'm not going to tell you anything anyway."

"Actually, you just told me everything."

"What?"

"You've been working for Romance for three years. When I asked you, you crossed your legs. In our brains there's a gland called the amygdala that regulates a lot of our emotional processes. To make a long story short, when you're lying or feeling a sense of discomfort, you scratch certain parts of your body or change your position in the chair as in your case. Your body answered my question, even though you remained silent. On the other hand, when I asked you if you freely chose to board the ship, you expressed contempt by twitching the corners of your mouth. So, in addition to judging that the question made you uncomfortable, it is clear that you came aboard to escape from something or someone, or more simply that you were not very happy about it. Shall I go on?"

"No, that's enough. You're right about everything. It's amazing what you can accomplish just by looking at someone. I wonder if you have any other hidden qualities. If you'd like maybe we can explore them together this evening..."

William didn't immediately realize what the woman meant, but then understood that she had just invited him to her cabin.

"I don't think so, Medea."

"OK, fine. It's a long trip, if you change your mind, let me know," she said with a wink and sashayed toward a corridor lit with red service lights.

Shaking his head, William sat there mulling it over. Once again, he examined the Latin inscription on the bottom of the plate. Who wanted to send him that message? Why use Latin?

Not long after, Madeline approached. William motioned for her to sit down. In a whisper, he said, "Move slowly and inconspicuously toward me and read the message engraved on the bottom of the plate."

"It's Latin, William. Your grandfather Walter knew Latin very well; he studied it in Italy during his years at university. Someday I'll tell you why he was able to feel emotions, but now's not the time for that. I barely remember Latin; can you translate it?"

"Yes, Grandfather Walter used to tell me stories by Phaedrus every night. My favorite was the one about Mercury and the sculptor. I've been studying Latin a lot recently, because of my teaching position at the university. I'm guessing you know how much I love history, right?"

"Well... of course," Madeline said but she was embarrassed: she didn't actually know that much about her son's life but she didn't want to show it.

"So, let me think. It can be translated as: *Blessed are those who have only one eye in the land of the blind,* and the two Roman numerals in the message are 21 and 4."

Once he cleaned the bottom of the plate better with some bread, he discovered a symbol depicting a circle with a triangle inside, which in turn enclosed a square and a smaller circle.

"Mother, what does this mean? Have you ever seen this symbol?"

"No, I have no idea, I've never seen it before."

Madeline had many things that she wanted to discuss with her son. Events had unfolded so quickly and she hadn't been able to tell him everything she wanted. It was a paradox: here she was, a mother full of remorse, who wanted to tell her son what had led her to make the wrong choices in the past, and yet she was talking about something else entirely. She had to begin somewhere.

5. The Depths of the Abyss

William and Madeline were still in the mess hall when she spoke again.

"I can't change the past, son, but I'm glad I have a chance to redeem myself. Your father was a true force of nature. When he set out to achieve a goal, nothing could stop him. Honestly, I was not the one who wanted him to die. But the time has come for me to make a confession. I know who is taking emotions away from human beings and I also know what their next move will be. What I am going to tell you, unfortunately, has to do with the Minedal-e Corporation pharmaceutical company."

She paused. Tears had filled her eyes and were flowing down her cheeks and between her lips. In order not to be overwhelmed by her emotions, she grabbed a glass of water from the table and drank it all in one go. Her heart was beating fast; she was ready to reveal the whole truth to her son.

"You already know the story of the Shelton Malthens, even if only in part." Madeline felt a strange tingling sensation at the tips of her toes, but she didn't pay much attention to it and continued. "Since the time of the first crusade, while many rulers fought among themselves to conquer new lands, a secret organization managed to grow disproportionately strong. Legend has it that the source of their power was contained in an object that could control people's emotions." Madeline felt her body temperature rising rapidly, so she loosened the first button of her blouse to relieve the pressure on her neck. She was having difficulty swallowing; she thought the unusual sensation was due to fatigue.

"Is this about the Templars, Mom? If I'm not mistaken, the last Grand Master was Jacques de Molay."

"Don't be ridiculous. There's always a lot of talk about the Templars, but it's just a way to put historians off the trail. Few know the history of a far more powerful organization, one that's not inspired by any religion. No such object has ever been found and, as a scientist, I can only say that it seems quite absurd to think that an artifact can magically control emotions."

"And yet, if it did exist," William spoke up, "just think what infinite power it would confer to its possessor. If two dictators wanted to go to war with each other, it would be enough for one of them to present this object to the other and all forms of anger would be eliminated and there would be no strife. Wars would be won in a flash."

"Don't let your imagination run away with you, my son. The history of MC did not begin in this century - or even the previous one..." Madeline coughed and brought her hands to her neck. She was having difficulty breathing and was gasping for breath. Before suddenly slumping to the ground, she managed to utter her final words: "The pinecone in front of the emperor's eyes and in his head..."

"Get the doctor!" William shouted to those present.

The sailors rushed over, forming a circle around the unconscious woman.

Acli, the ship's doctor, came running. A slender woman with pronounced features, her eyes moved quickly, taking in everything around her. She moved with confidence, demonstrating an ability to face and manage unexpected situations rationally. She grabbed Madeline's wrist, then placed two fingers on her jugular. "She's in danger! Bring a stretcher!"

William was not allowed to enter the infirmary so he waited across the hall to hear about his mother. When Acli opened the door, he sprang to his feet. The woman looked distraught. Her ash gray hair was messy and her eyes hid an inaccessible soul.

"Forgive me, but we haven't been introduced yet. My name is Acli and I'm the ship's doctor. By a miracle, Madeline is alive, but she has been poisoned. Unfortunately, I couldn't retrieve the glass that was on your table, otherwise I could have analyzed it."

"That was my glass. Maybe they were trying to poison me and not my mother!"

"I didn't know it was your mother! You'd better lock yourself in the cabin and don't open for anyone. Just give me time to write up the report for the captain."

Willy came rushing in. "What's going on, Acli?"

"They poisoned William's mother. Her condition is stable for now but I don't know if she'll make it through the night."

"Oh no! How terrible. There's a traitor on board," said the ship's captain. "I suggest we summon all crew members to the main deck. It won't be difficult for you to find the culprit by observing their body language and facial micro-expressions. What do you say, William?"

"It would be a predictable move: if their goal is to take me out, they will use the opportunity to act. I'm going to lock myself in the cabin. I need to think and then I'll let you know what we should do." Turning to the ship's doctor he said, "Be sure to let me know if my mother's condition worsens."

"Certainly, you can count on me."

William retreated to his cabin. He was still shaken by what had happened to his mother, so, in an effort to think of something else, he focused on the clues he had. The Latin phrase, whose translation seemed to have no connection with reality, still rang in his head: *Blessed are those who have only one eye in the land of the blind 21 - 4.* On one hand, this could be interpreted along the lines of "the mediocre look like geniuses among the ignorant" but it could also mean "be content with what you have." Then there were the Roman numerals XXI and IV. Could they be from a Bible verse or another sacred text? William felt entirely in the dark, unable to put the pieces of that difficult to decipher message together. He also thought back to Madeline's last words: "The pinecone in front of the emperor's eyes and in his head..." What on earth had she meant by that? Historically, no emperor had ever been depicted with a pinecone in front of his eyes; generally something more noble was used. The intent of a symbol was to relay the great deeds of a leader and enhance his image. At the moment he simply did not have enough information to solve this riddle.

The world seemed to have suddenly collapsed on William. He felt sad because his wife and son had disappeared. He imagined holding them tightly in his arms. Moreover, he hadn't been able to talk things over with his mother. He wished he could have learned more about her personality and, more importantly, what had led her to join forces with a criminal organization so many years ago. He still had mixed feelings about her: she was his mother and instinctively loved her, but he couldn't forget how much she had hurt him in the past. "There's a traitor on the ship and I must find out who it is!" he thought.

Sleep, disturbed by the sad events that happened to this reflective man, decided to blow its dust of dreams into the air, and William fell asleep.

The next morning, after a number of push-ups to maintain efficient muscle tone, he took a regenerative shower and quickly ate some fruit. With his pistol secured to his ankle and the other concealed under his black leather coat, he went to speak to the ship's captain.

"Willy, gather all the crew together please."

"I was just about to call you. I'm sorry but…"

"Willy! What happened?"

"Unfortunately, your mother didn't make it. I'm sorry, she passed away a few minutes ago."

William had experienced tragedy before, people close to him had died in the past, but this time, it was different; his heart was torn apart by grief. A tear, a shy vanguard of a vast army soon to follow, appeared. He decided not to say a word and retreated to his cabin to wait for the funeral service that would be held on the main deck of the ship.

That day, the sea was rough, and because of Madeline's death, so was the crew's mood. Her corpse lay inside a body bag on a special wooden table, supported on either side by two trestles. The entire crew had lined up to pay their last respects, the ship's engines had stopped roaring. William hoped that his mother would reappear suddenly, stepping out of a dark corner, and reveal that she was alive; he was used to her twists and turns. So, he walked over to the black bag and opened it. Unfortunately, his wishes vanished with the jarring sound of the zipper: Madeline really was dead. He gave her one last caress and motioned for the men to proceed. Brothers Karl and Jacob, aided by galley master Ephialtes and sailor Bill, tilted the table and the body slid overboard. Music from Orpheus' lyre was carried by the wind until it broke on the waves and was lost there, softening them. Marko, the Lieutenant

Commander, could hardly contain his emotion. Romance also seemed deeply upset: even though he had little sympathy for Madeline, his loyalty was genuine and he respected the head of Emosemvi and felt sad for him. Stan, Jack and Willy went to embrace their leader, who stood pensively to one side, in silence.

The ship's doctor approached. "I did everything I could to save your mother, but she ingested too much poison. I hope you can find the person responsible before we arrive in Europe."

"I appreciate everything you did for my mother. I will find the culprit; you can be sure of it."

The two siblings, Ephialtes and Medea, were the first to take their leave and return to their duties. The ship's engine roared to life, saluting Madeline one last time with three long blasts of the siren. The woman hadn't even had time to tell her son her secrets and now she had taken them with her to the bottom of the abyss.

A few days later, the entire crew was called to gather in the mess hall to be questioned by William. There was a strong smell of fish in the air. Evidently, Chef Jack was at work, cooking up one of his delicacies. Medea brought William a cup of coffee.

"Do you really think you'll be able to discover the culprit?" she asked in her smooth and persuasive manner.

"Certainly. The murderer doesn't stand a chance with me."

No sooner had William spoken these words than the sound of gunshot exploded in the air. Ephialtes had shot his gun into the air, then pointed the weapon at his sister, Medea, and at William. The woman quickly drew her pistol from the holster concealed under her uniform jacket and fired first, striking her brother dead. Incredulous, and in an obvious state of shock, she immediately dropped the gun and began to cry.

"I didn't mean to, it was instinctive..." she said.

Ephialtes gathered up his last ounces of energy before dying and uttered the words: "Medea, tell our father that..." and then he closed his eyes forever, cradled by the rocking of the ship.

The woman collapsed on the ground, unconscious. The ship's doctor rushed over and once she had established that Ephialtes was dead, she took Medea, with the help of Marko, to the infirmary. The action had happened so quickly that it left everyone present speechless.

"The traitor made a mistake," Romance said walking over to William.

"Yes, but I didn't expect it to end like this."

"He probably thought he was going to be caught. He was aware of your lie-detection skills. He feared being interrogated and committed an extreme act so that he wouldn't have to."

"I don't know, Romance. The name Ephialtes derives from the ancient Greek, it's the name of a man who betrayed his people. The sailor who just died, who had that same name, seems to have acted the same way. It feels bizarre, too much of a coincidence. Let's go see Medea.

Without her swift action, I wouldn't be here talking to you. She saved my life."

When they arrived at the infirmary they found Acli, Captain Willy and Medea talking among themselves. Medea was crying. "I never thought I would have to kill my brother! He's always been stubborn. If only he had listened to me..."

"You saved my life and I want to thank you. We have both lost loved ones in a very short space of time. What can you tell me about Ephialtes? Who or what drove him to kill my mother? Why did he want me dead?"

"I don't know. We didn't talk much. He was always obsessed with legends about sects and secret fraternities. Maybe he was hired by your enemies. Other than that, I don't know. Now excuse me, but I really don't feel like talking."

"I understand. I'm upset about losing my mother, too..."

"Yes, but I killed my brother!" the woman screamed at him through her tears.

William nodded and headed back to his cabin in order to reflect on what had happened. If Ephialtes was the traitor, who had hired him? Who had written the message in Latin that was hidden on the bottom of the plate? It could not have been Ephialtes. With these questions still in his mind, he entered his cabin and locked himself inside. He tried to get some rest, but he couldn't get the image of his mother, who had just perished, out of his mind.

6. A Look at the Sky

The following day, the body of Ephialtes sunk to the bottom of the abyss. The funeral ceremony, though less solemn than Madeline's, also took place on the main deck. After several days of navigation, the Elpis docked at the port of Civitavecchia, also known as the "Port of Rome."

Lieutenant Commander Marko personally handled the administrative procedures with the port authorities, while William and his Emosemvi companions boarded a van that took them to the Bona Fide Hotel in Rome. Driving the van was Valerio, an employee of Rotaon Ltd, who worked in the Italian port. He had been handling business for Romance for years and was an expert in loading delicate cargo onto ships. Lately he had been loading narcotic substances contained inside fragile glass vials, used by zoos to put animals to sleep. Romance now handled all kinds of merchandise and his business was booming. Generous and altruistic, the proceeds of his business went towards helping the homeless of Happiness

City through a foundation managed by James, a member of Emosemvi.

Strangely enough, Valerio's face was expressionless, as if he couldn't feel any emotions: he spoke little and often stared off into space. Romance did not pay much attention to it, attributing the attitude of his employee to fatigue from his intense work.

On leaving the port, neither the security systems nor the customs guards checked the identity of the people inside the van, nor did they conduct any inspections. Evidently Romance had some influential friends.

The traffic was quite congested and the sounds were deafening.

"Some things never change; I love everything about Rome, including its flaws," William thought as he looked out the van window at the shops. He noticed the sign of a bakery; a distant memory, like a barely perceptible echo, crossed his mind. Many years before, during one of his trips to Rome, he had stopped to buy a sandwich in a small store. The clerk had sliced some ham and stuffed it inside a rosette, a crispy roll of bread whose shape vaguely resembled a star with a bulge in the middle. Both the intense flavor of the food and the fact that he had eaten it in Italy, the undisputed global home of food, left him with an excellent memory. Returning to Rome was like diving into the past, into traditions and history.

As soon as the van ventured through the streets of the center of town, another memory took shape in William's mind. Before the disappearance of emotions, on practically every street, you could find a roasted chestnut vendor; they put the chestnuts in a cone-shaped piece of brown paper and sold them to passers-by. The inhabitants of the city didn't pay much attention to the vendors, but their presence, especially in the eyes of tourists, added atmosphere to the city. Now, with people unable to appreciate flavors, it was sad to see the good food going unsold.

When they arrived at the hotel, which was located in the heart of Rome, at the intersection of two narrow streets where they seemed to be able to breathe in the history of the city, they noticed that the faces of all the passers-by were ice cold. No one expressed any emotion. All conversations took place in low voices, with no emphatic words or comments. This was very unusual for Italians, who are known for their lively temperaments and talkativeness.

The Bona Fide Hotel was small. From the outside it looked no different than a private home, except that it had thirty-four decorative banners hanging from each window sill. The peculiarity of that hotel, which was once a popular destination for tourists because of its central location, was precisely those red forked banners: at night, when the lights came on, they were illuminated and looked like fiery tongues. Especially in the winter, when the wind blew fast through the narrow alleyways, the banners waved frantically, as if they had come to life, making a strange sound and giving rise to the legend that the banners were the tongues of the damned, people in hell, who wanted nothing more than to tell their sad stories.

William headed towards the reception desk, looking around, trying to take in every little detail. The environment was formal, decorated with staid and elegant furnishings, and pastoral landscapes hung on the walls. But what made the lobby especially unique was its vaulted ceiling and the large fresco of the Archangel Michael in the act of chasing away the rebellious angels.

When he reached the reception desk, which was decorated in red, white, yellow and black, William couldn't believe his eyes. Bringlux, the owner of the odd hotel in Surprise City, the one that had the shape of an inverted funnel, stood before him in an elegant black suit and white tie.

"We meet again, William," the man said, winking at him, his eyes smoldering like embers.

"I remember you well. You helped Emosemvi a great deal in the past. What are you doing working here?"

Bringlux stroked his neatly combed back black hair and pursed his red lips. "Although time has passed, you still ask the most obvious questions. But allow me to satisfy your curiosity. When emotions returned, thanks to Emosemvi's intervention, business at my hotel in Surprise City did exceptionally well. So, I decided to hand over the keys to an associate and move here for work." Leaning across the counter, so as not to be heard by others, he added, "No one here feels emotions anymore; something strange has happened. I don't know how they did it, but from one day to the next, everything changed. It didn't happen gradually. No one can seem to find a plausible explanation. Even the newspapers aren't talking about it – the journalists here have all turned into soulless automatons."

Just then, a customer wearing an elegant felt hat approached to pick up the key to his room. Bringlux, suspecting him of being a spy, stood to attention and started speaking about a trivial matter in a loud voice. "What do you think of the fresco, William? I commissioned it myself, you know... I do enjoy a bit of irony." With a polite smile he then handed the key to the man in the felt hat, greeted him cordially as he walked away, and went on.

"Listen to me carefully, William. I'm not going to stand here and tell you the usual legends about the Templars and other orders of chivalry, but I do want to tell you one thing. At the time of the first crusade in 1099, after the siege of Jerusalem, while all the victors were intent on dividing up the booty plundered from the newly conquered city, four mysterious knights stole an artifact that had been kept in its dungeons. The knights, riding four horses of different colors, reached a secret place to the north of Jerusalem in seven days and hid the object there. With the passing of time, the power granted to these knights by the artifact allowed them to accumulate great wealth and new followers. Thus, an organization came into being that was given the name of MC. Contrary to popular belief, these are neither the initials of the Minedal-e Corporation nor an anagram of your mother's name, Madeline, but the year the secret organization was established. In fact, in Roman numerals, the letter "M" means "1000", while the "C" stands for the number "100" If we put the two letters together we get the year 1100, the year after the Crusaders took Jerusalem... But let's be clear, I was very young at that time!" Bringlux interrupted himself for a moment to smile and laugh at his own joke. Then he grew serious again. A strange light in his eyes seemed to blaze like an untamable flame, as he concluded his tale: "The purpose of this organization is simple. It wants to take over the world and gain domination of it. I that is, we cannot allow it. Over the centuries, the mysterious object I mentioned seems to have been used to win numerous wars and only those who swore obedience to MC could access its immense power. Moreover, the Grand Master of this organization is still alive and seems to be a descendant of one of the four founding knights of MC. He protects and safeguards this object carefully and nobody knows what it looks like."

William couldn't believe the tale he had just heard. It was surreal, it had to be a legend. How could Bringlux expect a rational person like him, however passionate about ancient history he might be, to actually believe it?

"Thank you for telling me this fantastic story. Maybe one day someone will make a movie out of it. I like history, but I really prefer not to believe in legends. Right now, I'm only interested in finding my son, Virgil, and my wife, Beatrice."

"I never asked you to believe me, but I thought it was only fair that I should open a window onto the world that your rational mind won't let you enter. Take a walk around the hotel and you'll find what you're looking for: you may be able to save your family."

Bringlux already seemed to be aware of Beatrice and Virgil's abduction. William had been able to trust the man in the past, and as mysterious as he was, he was certainly not a traitor.

Bringlux cleared his throat and returned to being an efficient hotel receptionist. "Your room is number 100 and it is located on the third floor. As for your friends, don't worry, I will give them all comfortable rooms. Enjoy your stay."

Heading for the elevator, William told his companions to get ready, that he would probably call them in for a briefing shortly. Upon reaching his room he noted that it was quite large and had a rosewood four-poster bed situated in the center. "I like the streaks of black in the wood and its sweet smell, rosewood, my favorite," he thought while observing the room. He had just started unpacking when there was a knock at the door. He pulled out his gun to avoid being caught off guard. At the door stood Medea.

"Hello William, may I come in?"

"What are you doing here? I didn't expect to see you. I just arrived and was about to unpack."

"Don't worry, I won't bite. It will only take a moment. I need to talk to you. After all, I saved your life, didn't I?"

He nodded and let the woman enter. She wore a tight black suit and as usual moved sinuously. Letting down her long black hair, she said, "I won't bother you and feel free to act as you see fit. But, after saving your life, I think I've earned a place in Emosemvi, don't you? I've been on the Elpis for too long. My brother was my only family, and now I have to rebuild my life. I don't have a lot of places where I can go, but I do have a degree in history and maybe there's some way I could be of help."

"I don't know..." he replied, feeling somewhat embarrassed. On the one hand, he didn't want to close the door in the face of the person who had saved his life, on the other hand he wanted to keep Medea away from him because, although he loved Beatrice above all else, he didn't want to be near a woman who could upset his soul and lead him into temptation.

"Alright Medea, get a room in the hotel and make yourself available."

"I already have. As it happens, they've given me room 101, right next to yours."

"Ah, I see," William said.

"Yes," she said, looking him straight in the eye.

"Well, you can go now. Eventually I'll call everyone for a briefing," he said in a hurry and opened the door, glancing down the hall to avoid her gaze.

She disappeared into her room, leaving behind a trail of sweet and fruity perfume that gave William a headache.

The afternoon passed and after an invigorating shower William decided to follow Bringlux's advice and go for a walk. He left the hotel and headed to a bar to enjoy a coffee *granita* with whipped cream. While his head was swirling with thoughts, he heard someone say his name. It was Medea. She was standing there in a green dress with thin purple straps. The dress was very flattering on her, and her eyes were of the same color.

"Are you following me, Medea?"

"No, I just happened to be here, but if you want I'll leave."

"So many coincidences. First you're in the room next to mine, and now we bump into each other at the bar."

"Isn't all of life a coincidence, William? Anyway, let's get down to business. Are you doing some research?"

He didn't know whether he should reveal what he was looking for or not. But then he concluded that perhaps he could use a hand. After all, she had saved his life and he felt indebted to her for it.

"I have one clue. It's a phrase in Latin that I found on the bottom of a plate when we were aboard Elpis."

"I know Latin, I studied it in school."

"You surprise me, Medea, I didn't think you were so well-read."

"I have many hidden talents..."

"Alright... now let's focus on the Latin phrase: *Beati monoculi in terra caecorum XXI - IV*. That is, "*Blessed are those who have only one eye in the land of the blind, 21 - 4.*" I can't even figure out the meaning of these Roman numerals."

"It's an ancient Latin motto, William. Of course, living with one eye can't be easy."

"What was that?" William asked suddenly, smacking his forehead in amazement.

"I said it's an ancient Latin motto."

"No, no, repeat what you said after that!"

"Living with one eye can't be easy."

William hastily rummaged through his pockets, pulled out a coin and left it on the counter next to his icy drink. Thanking the barman, he hurried out of the bar, followed by Medea.

"Where are we going, William?"

"Blessed are those who have only one eye in the land of the blind...One eye, that's it!" He stopped short as he pointed with his finger to the majestic monument of the Pantheon. "On the top of the dome is a circular opening called an oculus. That's the eye we're looking for!"

"Of course!" exclaimed the woman.

"You see, Medea, the eye not only brings light into the building, it allows Catholics to pray while gazing at the sky."

"Here I must correct you, William. This is not a building for people of the Catholic faith. In Greek *pan* means *all*, while *theon* means *gods*. Therefore, this monument is dedicated to all the gods."

"In ancient times, you're right, Medea, but the Pantheon was converted into a Christian church, and now it is called *Santa Maria ad Martyres*. Mass is regularly celebrated here."

"Touché."

"I beg your pardon?"

"You're showing off your education, but next time watch out. I'm competitive! I like to win."

"Medea, this is not a contest to see who is more educated. Let's go now. I don't want to waste any more time."

The two of them walked under the colonnade and crossed the threshold through the large bronze door.

"I suggest, Medea, that you do not show the slightest emotion. If your face even hints at an expression, the custodian or any other person could alert the men of MC."

"Alright, got it. I'll be careful."

The majesty of the Pantheon left them speechless. They stood looking up, contemplating the dome and its circular opening through which they could see white clouds with golden flecks.

It was William who spoke first. "The message found at the bottom of the plate on the ship, in addition to the Latin phrase, also contained two numbers: 21 and 4. My mother's last words were: *The pinecone in front of the emperor's eyes and in his head.* Let's look around for some kind of sign, numbers or a clue that could put us on track."

The two spent several hours scouring the entire building but found nothing. The sun's rays, now weary of lighting the earth, were retreating in search of rest. The custodian of the building invited the few people there to get ready to leave, as it was almost closing time. Since emotions had been removed from the world, the monuments were not as crowded as they once were, and the Pantheon was no longer a popular destination.

Before leaving, William turned one last time to look at the dome, disappointed not to have found what he was looking for. He closed his eyes, as if he wanted to concentrate and breathe in the history of that building. After a few minutes, he exclaimed, "Rome's birthday! How did I not think of it before!"

Medea didn't quite understand what he meant at first. "Whose birthday?" Then she understood. "It's a date, of course!" She clenched her fists tightly, trying to hold back her growing emotions.

"According to legend, Romulus, the first king of Rome supposedly founded the city on April 21, 753 BC. The numbers in the message found on the bottom of the plate refer to that date: twenty-one is the day and four is the month, which is to say, April. You surely know that one day a year, on April 21st at noon, the sun shines straight through the oculus hitting the exact center of the front door. That was when the emperor crossed the threshold of the building and his body was bathed in light. So, my mother, with her last words, meant that the pinecone is in front of the emperor's eyes. If the emperor was right here at the entrance where we are now, it means that the symbol of the pinecone is somewhere inside the building and could be right in front of us. But where? We searched for hours and didn't find anything."

The custodian told them it was time to leave, but William had no intention of leaving. He was close to solving the puzzle.

"William, I think we need to leave. The custodian is staring at us."

"Don't worry, just give me a moment. He can't feel anger anyway."

"Perhaps the pinecone symbol was removed and there's nothing here. There's a crazy draft in here and it's cold as hell - can we leave now?" Medea asked, shifting her weight from one foot to the other, to warm herself up.

"You've done it again! I'm beginning to wonder if you're doing it on purpose," William said in surprise.

"What did I do?"

"You just gave me an idea where the pinecone is. Repeat what you just said, please."

"I said it's cold as hell and..."

"Exactly! Initially, the Pantheon was built as a temple dedicated to the deities of many religions. As I told you, it was later converted into a Christian church. On the day of the consecration, Catholic prelates entered this building for the first time. According to legend, during the ceremony, the seven pagan demons that inhabited these walls up until that moment fled. On top of the dome was a large pinecone that was like a kind of cork. One of the demons, very similar to the devil, apparently hit it with his horns, making it fall so he could escape. The pinecone fell not far from here, in a place that was later called, "Piazza della Pigna." My mother was referring to the pinecone that, according to legend, plugged up the oculus and was placed in front of the emperor."

"You really are clever! Bravo, together we make quite a pair! Is the pinecone a legend or does it really exist?"

"It really exists. It's a large bronze sculpture and was discovered not far from here."

"So, let's not waste time looking for a symbol, let's find this work of art! Let's go to Piazza della Pigna now!" Medea said emphatically.

"Actually, it would be useless, because the pinecone was later taken to the Vatican, that is our next destination."

The custodian stood there watching them in silence. The two of them walked away and headed back to the hotel. The streets of the city were deserted and the wind sang its song, whistling through the alleys, looking for faces to caress. Since emotions had left the world, people were no longer interested in going to public places, they preferred to stay at home instead. The red forked banners fluttered frantically that evening, creating a special welcome for William and Medea.

7. Reality or Legend?

Romance was waiting in the lobby, restlessly pacing back and forth. As soon as he saw William he ran towards him and after looking around to make sure he wasn't heard by anyone, he said, "Bad news unfortunately."

"What's going on?"

"I managed to get in touch with old Tobia, but things aren't going well. As you ordered, they have set up an operations room at Gear Jesture and can easily get in touch with us while also providing us with logistical support."

"That sounds good. So, what's the bad news?"

"It's about the emotions. All across Anger City and in neighboring cities, emotions are vanishing from people. The world is changing again. No one can explain how in such a short time people's faces have taken on neutral expressions. Maggie, for example, was standing in the checkout line of a supermarket with a friend and laughing with her about something funny that had happened recently when, all of a sudden, the friend started staring at

Maggie with an expressionless face and icy eyes. Several people around them also stopped showing emotion and their faces took on the same neutral expression."

"That is indeed strange: it can't be a serum then, because it's not being administered to them in public, and especially not at the same time to all those people," said William, puzzled.

"I don't believe in legends, much less curses, but could it have something to do with that mysterious object found in Jerusalem that Bringlux was talking about?"

"How did you know about that?" William asked, looking Romance up and down from head to toe.

"Well, while you were out, he told me the strange legend - there may be some truth in it."

"Bringlux should think about doing his job and talking less. Anyway, there's no magical object that can remove emotions from human beings."

At that precise moment, a man wearing a purple-colored hooded cape walked hastily out of the hotel, leaving a leather briefcase on the lobby floor. Bringlux noticed it, and rushed over, picked it up and attempted to run after the man in the street to return it to him. As soon as he passed through the front door, there was a loud explosion, and the shock waves not only shattered the window panes, but also threw William, Romance and Medea to the ground, stunning them for a few seconds.

Stan, Willy, Jack, and Orpheus, who were in a nearby room, rushed into the lobby to help their comrades.

"Are you alright? Are you injured?" Stan asked with concern.

"A man wearing a hooded cape...chase him down, he just left...Bringlux, I don't think he survived...go!" said William with difficulty, visibly shocked at what had happened.

Medea and Romance were fine, even if their clothes had been torn in several places, while there was a strong smell of smoke in the lobby from a scorched corner of the large oriental carpet. A tornado seemed to have whipped through the hall: some of the furniture had been thrown a few feet by the shock wave and pieces of the transparent reception desk were scattered on the floor.

Jack and Orpheus chased after the bomber through the alleys of the city in the direction of the Pantheon, while Stan and Willy went in the opposite direction, hoping to find this mysterious person, who seemed to have simply vanished. Jack and Orpheus ran through the streets; just when they had lost all hope of finding the bomber, they spotted him running like the wind down Via delle Muratte in the direction of the Trevi Fountain. He was fast, did not seem to tire at all and was getting further and further away from them, while his pursuers were exhausted and couldn't gain ground. They turned right on Via delle Quattro Fontane, reached the Papal Basilica of Santa Maria Maggiore, and then turned onto Piazza Vittorio Emanuele II. The mysterious man clambered over a fence and seemed to be caught in a dead end. In front of him there was a walled doorway with a marble frame and some strange symbols engraved on it. He had no escape. Soon they would catch up to him. Orpheus drew his gun, but just when he was about to reach the mysterious man, he vanished into thin air, swallowed up by the shadows of the evening.

"We've lost him!" exclaimed Orpheus.

"He can't have vanished into thin air," said Jack as he walked towards the door, noting that it was actually walled up. The mysterious man could never have gone through it. On either side of the door were two statues of ancient gods, while above was a large marble disk, with two inverted triangles and a circle with a cross over it. Still panting from the chase, Orpheus doubled over, hands on his knees to catch his breath, when he noticed an object glittering in the grass. It was a small golden cross with a red rose in the center.

"Maybe he dropped it," he thought. He picked up the object and put it in his pocket.

In the meantime, William, Medea and Romance slowly recovered. Except for an annoying whistling in their ears, they had not suffered any injuries. At the time of the explosion, there were no customers in the lobby and the fire alarm had gone off almost immediately. Flashing police lights sounded outside the hotel. Just as William started to reflect on the life of Bringlux and mourn his death, the hotelier walked through the front door. He didn't have a single scratch; his hair was neatly combed and his suit was impeccable.

"I hope you weren't frightened," Bringlux said quietly as if nothing unusual had happened.

"I thought you were dead..."

"Don't be silly. Either you underestimate me, William, or you've given up and aren't using your wits any more. My associates will take care of the formalities with the police and reassure the customers. In the meantime, follow me."

He headed down a wood-paneled, doorless hallway and walked into a well-lit room; inside was a large rectangular table and twelve chairs, each with a colored stone set into the back of the seat. Bringlux invited those present to sit down.

"In the past I helped you restore emotions to the world," Bringlux said solemnly. "When a human being is deprived of emotions, it is as their souls had been emptied out, and we cannot let this happen. The world has always survived its destiny throughout the millennia because good and evil have always been in balance. I will help you restore emotions this time, too, but you will face great dangers and I don't know how many of you will survive."

Just then, Stan, Willy, Jack and Orpheus entered the room on their way back from the mission. Orpheus tossed the small golden cross with the red rose in its center onto the table.

"We lost him, unfortunately. We only managed to find this. The man seemed to vanish in front of a door. From a distance it looked like he was walking through it, but it was bricked up."

William picked up the object to examine it, then handed it to Bringlux. "It's the Rosicrucian Order, if I'm not mistaken."

Bringlux nodded, though without touching the cross. "You're the history expert here, enlighten us."

Everyone there looked at each other, shaking their heads. They had no idea what the two men were talking about.

"I don't see how this has anything to do with emotions and their disappearance," William began. "But in any case, the Rosicrucian is a secret order founded around 1400, although some scholars claim it originated much earlier, in the days of ancient Rome. In 17th century Germany an anonymous booklet titled *Fama fraternitatis Rosae Crucis* was in circulation that spoke of the life of a certain Christian Rosenkreuz or "Christian Rosicrucian," who would have been one of the Grand Masters of this order. One hundred and twenty years after his death, his body was found intact and surrounded by strange symbols. The order is inspired by Christian ideals combined with Egyptian myths. Legend has it that illustrious figures such as Galileo, Da Vinci, Bacon, Shakespeare, Descartes and others all belonged to it."

Everyone turned to look at each other in amazement.

"Orpheus may have managed to chase that mysterious man all the way to the Alchemical door in Piazza Vittorio Emanuele II," Medea added.

William shot her a look. "How do you know that door?" he asked quizzically.

"Well, it's a famous tourist spot in Rome. It would be strange if I didn't know about it…"

William nodded, "All right, let's move on. Engraved on the door are symbols of the planets associated with metals. For example, Saturn is paired with lead, Jupiter with tin, Mars with iron. These are classic illustrations found in many textbooks of alchemy that were common in the 1600s, and on the door you can also find the seal of gold and the sun that nowadays is still printed on the banknotes of some countries."

"All we needed was a magic door!" exclaimed Jack, rubbing his bald head and smoothing down his thick black beard.

William paid no attention to his comment and continued.

"That door was one of the entrances to a now-demolished villa owned by Massimiliano Savelli Palombara, Marquis of Pietraforte, a friend of Queen Christina of Sweden, with whom he shared a passion for alchemy. The Marquis was a member of the Rosicrucians and in the basement of his villa there was an alchemical laboratory, where he conducted his experiments. The Roman historian Francesco Girolamo Cancellieri wrote, in one of his works, about the legend of a pilgrim who was hosted in the villa of Marquis Palombara. During the night he worked in the alchemical laboratory, managing to create gold from nothing. At the first light of the morning the pilgrim was seen disappearing through the Alchemical Door, leaving behind small gold filaments and a mysterious manuscript full of magical symbols and enigmatic puzzles. A few years ago, at my university, I was conducting a study on ancient inscriptions and I happened to come across a copy of Cancellieri's text. In addition to reporting every detail about the life of the Marquis, it had illustrations that showed the epigraphs in the villa before they were irreparably destroyed."

"What do the Rosicrucians want from us? How are they involved with the disappearance of emotions?" asked Stan with curiosity.

"I do not know, really. The story of the Rosicrucians is a legend. No one has ever been able to prove the existence of this supposed secret order and, as I told Bringlux in the hotel lobby, I believe in science and not in magical rituals and alchemical doors."

Medea decided to step in and state her point of view. In a firm tone, without a shadow of hesitation, she said, "If the order is secret, it is normal that no one has ever revealed its existence. I would not underestimate the power in the hands of the Grand Master and his members."

"Alright, Medea, I want to be open minded," William replied. "I have learned to question everything in life, even my deepest beliefs. So, tomorrow morning - if the hotel has not suffered any structural damage and the police allow us to spend the night here - we will continue our search for the truth. But first, I order everyone not to show the slightest sign of emotion. Don't let your facial expressions betray you. Enemies are everywhere and they could discover you literally in the blink of an eye. So, when you talk to someone, keep your tone of voice monotone and your expressions neutral. Stan will be contacting our base of operations at Gear Jesture tomorrow morning to get the team to do some research and figure out how and why emotions are leaving people there as well. Stan, Willy, Orpheus, and Jack will travel to the Cortile della Pigna, located in the Vatican Museums complex, tomorrow morning. There's a bronze sculpture about 13 foot-tall that depicts a pinecone that was found in the Middle Ages not far from here and later moved to the Vatican. Legend has it that a demon struck a pinecone and it fell near the Pantheon. Take lots of photographs of the sculpture and note down every little detail. Romance and Medea and I will examine the Alchemical Door, or Magic Door as it's often called, to gather as many clues as possible. Any questions?"

Everyone nodded without adding anything. Bringlux informed them that the hotel had not suffered any structural damage. They could rest there without worry. Moreover, a police patrol unit had been stationed directly outside the Bona Fide.

Darkness swallowed up the alleys of Rome, plunging the city into silence with only the sound of the thirty-four tongue-like red banners fluttering in the wind outside the hotel.

PART TWO

The Message in the Symbols

1. The Door of Time

The next morning William got up early, did a few sets of crunches, and after showering and shaving, got dressed to go out. He didn't want to let any painful memories make their way into his mind, knowing that they would distract him. He needed to keep his mental resources on alert so that he could deal with whatever unexpected events the day would throw at him. However, he couldn't help thinking about his father and how much he would have loved to have him by his side. His father would surely have been able to guide him towards the solution of every puzzle using his wisdom and drawing on his vast learning. In truth, although William could not afford to show his companions the slightest sign of weakness, he felt terribly lonely. He was quite good at coming up with a plan or improvising in dangerous situations, but he was still a man, with both merits and flaws; he was beginning to get tired of all the action and just wanted to lead a normal life.

"Who knows if I'll ever be able to embrace my family again," he thought wistfully as he made his way down to the hotel lobby.

The two Emosemvi groups headed off to their respective destinations. Before leaving the hotel, Stan called his companions at Gear Jesture, and asked them to look into why humans were losing their emotions there as well.

As soon as they reached Piazza Vittorio Emanuele II, William's group found themselves in front of an iron fence, which they had to sneak over in order to be able to examine the Alchemical Door. Seen from close up, it was disturbing: many strange and arcane symbols and Latin inscriptions were depicted on it, while on the side two grotesque-looking white statues stood like sentries.

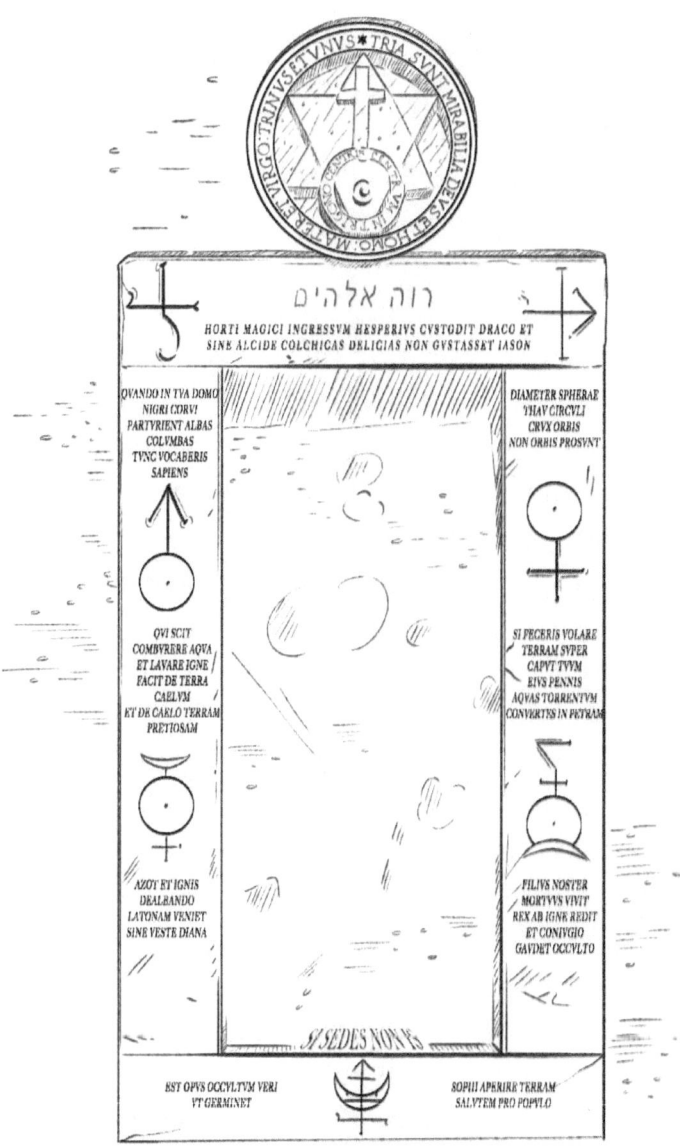

Alchemical Door located in Piazza Vittorio Emanuele II - Rome

"These statues did not belong to Marquis Palombara's villa. They were added at a later date and depict the Egyptian deity, Bes," William said.

Romance shook his head out of amazement; he wasn't a history expert and preferred to act as a lookout in case someone tried to surprise them.

Medea took a few pictures of the door, behind which stood a solid wall.

"William, our mystery man couldn't possibly have gone through the wall."

"Obviously not, but we need to sift through every detail to find out who he was, and more importantly, figure out why he was trying to kill us."

After carefully examining the door, without discovering any useful clues, they got ready to call it quits. The Latin inscriptions seemed to make no sense, and while the symbols were interpretable, they provided no concrete clues as to the identity of the mysterious man. When all hope seemed to have vanished, just like the bomber had, William noticed something at the base of the door. On the threshold, partly hidden by the wall and therefore barely visible, was the following Latin inscription: *si sedes non is.*

"Medea, can you translate that?"

"Let me examine it, William. Hmm, let's see. It could be *if you sit, you do not proceed,* right?"

"Yes, it's a palindrome, albeit not exactly identically readable from left to right."

"Meaning?" asked Medea in curiosity.

"If we read it from left to right it is *si sedes non is* and your translation *if you sit, you do not proceed* is correct. If, on the other hand, we read it from right to left, it says *si non sedes is* and that is *if you do not sit, you proceed.*"

"What does it mean, William?"

"Clearly it's an urging to continue looking. We need to reflect. Let us imagine that a person who lived several centuries ago stood before this door. *If you sit, you do not proceed* could mean: if you stand still and do not go through the door you will not be able to join us. As soon as you walked out of the door you would read the reverse inscription *if you do not sit, you proceed* meaning something like: if you do not stay with us then you are free to leave."

"OK, I get it, but how does this help us?"

"I need a moment to think."

Meanwhile a police car had stopped about fifty yards away from them. Two fully armed uniformed officers got out of it. It wasn't clear whether they were really cops or MC goons, but they had to hurry because the two men were approaching them, looking around circumspectly. Romance urged his companions to make it fast. The agents would soon be there.

"Medea, I think I understand," William said hastily. "The Latin phrase is an exhortation to continue the search for truth. We need to get through the door."

"Um...ok, but it's walled up and we can't get through it."

"I can see that. Of course, it's walled up, but you have to be able to grasp the metaphorical meaning. We must go through the door, which is to say we have to follow the footsteps of its owner. If we stay here contemplating it, we will never reach the truth. This is the sense of the Latin phrase: besides being a clear exhortation to take action, it is also an invitation to continue with our research. The villa is no longer there. Only the door was left, witness to so much history. But as I mentioned when we were in the hotel, the Roman historian Francesco Girolamo Cancellieri described the villa in detail in his book – there were several epigraphs, too, that are now lost. We must find that ancient text: reading it will bring us closer to the truth."

Romance rushed over, urging his two companions to follow him. The police officers were getting closer. So, they fled, climbed over the fence and rushed down an alley. The officers pursued them, but soon lost track of them because the narrow streets of the city were like a maze.

In the meantime, Stan, Willy, Jack and Orpheus walked into the Vatican Museums and headed towards the Cortile della Pigna. In the past, tourists used to have to wait for hours to visit it, forming a line along the perimeter of the Vatican walls, but now there wasn't even a soul around. Nobody seemed to be interested in art anymore.

The large pinecone, flanked by two bronze peacocks, was positioned on a capital at the top of a double flight of stairs. The group was taking detailed photos of the sculpture, even climbing up to see it better, when a man in a blue suit came forward and stopped in the middle of the courtyard. Orpheus signaled to his companions not to move. He walked towards the mysterious figure, noticing that he didn't look at all like a tourist.

"Orpheus! Legendary member of Emosemvi! What an honor!" the man in the elegant suit exclaimed.

"Have we met?"

"Not directly, but you are something of a celebrity after you helped William save the world."

"Is there something I can help you with?"

"No but maybe I can help you by freeing you from the bondage of emotion. MC is grateful to you."

The man pulled out a pinecone-shaped object from his pocket and showed it to Orpheus for a moment. Then he whispered a few words, after which he turned and headed for the exit. Orpheus stared at him as he walked away. Jack came up to him.

"Who was that guy?" he asked.

Orpheus stared at the exit and couldn't say a word.

"Hey, are you awake, Orpheus? I asked you who that guy was!" Jack repeated, raising the tone of his voice.

As if awakened from sleep and without any expression at all, Orpheus looked at him and said, "I don't know him, he said something about MC. I don't want to talk about it. We've done enough for today, let's leave."

"What are you saying? Are you crazy? We have to complete our mission!"

His gaze lost in the void and with no emotion on his face, Orpheus replied, "I think I'm done here."

Jack grabbed him by the shoulders and shook him vigorously, but his friend looked like a puppet and did not react. Concerned by the scene they were witnessing from afar, Stan and Willy rushed over.

"Orpheus is acting strangely," said Jack when they asked what was going on.

Stan passed a hand in front of Orpheus's glassy eyes, noticing that his friend showed no reaction, not even a blink of an eye. "Orpheus, what did that man have in his hand?"

With a monotonous tone and a blank look, Orpheus replied. "He was holding a pinecone. A beautiful object. And now I'm a free man."

The strange object had robbed Orpheus of all emotion.

The men of Emosemvi had just witnessed the power of the artifact that Bringlux had told William about, the same object that had been in the hands of a secret organization for thousands of years. Although they didn't want to believe in the magic, at the moment there seemed to be no other explanation for what had just happened.

Stan, Willy, and Jack looked at each other in puzzlement and decided to return to the hotel, accompany their friend to his room, and wait for their leader.

2. A Life for Emosemvi

Meanwhile back at Gear Jesture in Anger City, Maggie and her husband Seamus, were going over some old books on the Resistance Code, based on the interpretation of facial micro-expressions.

"While most facial expressions last more than a second, micro-expressions, on the other hand, last about 1/5th to 1/25th of a second. How can we possibly tell if someone is part of the Resistance?" Seamus asked, turning to his wife.

After some thought, she replied: "Resistance members use our code so that they can be recognized through speech. First of all, they express themselves using words referring to an emotional state, such as 'I am sad' or 'I despise that person' or 'that music makes me happy'. A member of the Resistance makes facial micro-expressions as he says these phrases, and if you notice them, it means you can trust him." Satisfied with her explanation, she added, "People who don't have emotions aren't able to pick up on facial micro-expressions."

"Well, Maggie, we are among the few left in town who do feel emotions and we can be detected easily, so let's be cautious. When we leave here, no smiles or angry expressions, OK?"

Right then, the metal rolling shutter of the body shop opened and James and Tobia rushed in. "We've got some important information!" exclaimed James, pulling back his long white hair.

After drinking a glass of water, James looked around the room, and then went on in a rush. "You won't even be able to guess what happened to us. We were with Tobia having something to eat at Somtlose, that place in Sadness City that the Inklings once ran...."

"Wasn't it blown up?" Maggie interrupted.

"Yes, but it was rebuilt and it has become a sort of shrine to the Resistance. Inside are lots of pictures of the former owner, Tisiphone, who died in the explosion. If you remember, William was almost killed there when the place blew up."

"Poor girl," Seamus added with a hint of sadness in his voice for the death of Tisiphone.

"Yes, she became a martyr for the Resistance. So, anyway, we were there and we witnessed an incredible scene. Next to us were lots of people with expressionless faces and empty eyes. There was also a couple, a pair of sweethearts, sitting in the back corner, gently teasing each other. At one point, a woman in a nurse's uniform came in. She had black hair pulled up in a tight bun on her head and a bizarre tattoo on her wrist. She walked up to the couple, showed them a pinecone-shaped object and then walked out. Those two kids, who were so full of life before, all of a sudden had a glassy look; they stopped being lovey-dovey and didn't even talk to each other anymore."

"Incredible!" exclaimed Maggie, then added emphatically, "Our enemies have something dangerous in their hands. It's amazing, it looks almost like one of those magical objects described in books of Greek mythology."

Old Tobia was listening to the conversation through his ear trumpet. "Send a message to William electronically and tell him what is happening. Then contact all Resistance sympathizers and put them on alert. They need to report anything unusual they notice in town. James and I will go to the old music building in Calicraston Ville, where there seems to be a strange coming and going of people. We need to find out what is going on. Hopefully our spies there passed us the right information."

Seamus and Maggie quickly got to work with the computers and radio equipment, while Tobia and James headed off in the car towards Calicraston Ville. The sun had now made room in the sky for the stars. A strange, cold and penetrating wind blew ominously, as if bringing bad news.

During the trip there, James felt nervous. In an attempt to contain his growing anxiety, he began to observe the surrounding countryside.

"What beautiful cottages! Someday I'll buy a piece of land and farm it, too," he thought. The nocturnal landscape was like a balm for his mood; it brought him a sense of relaxation and also triggered many thoughts. "I've made lots of mistakes in life but the only right thing I've done was to join Emosemvi. Everyone is entitled to a second chance. Yes, as soon as everything is over I will start a family and move out to the country." James was no hero: he had spent much of his life living on the streets due to lack of money and had accumulated debt. When one day Emosemvi recruited him, he decided to contribute by bringing emotions back to human beings.

Tobia, meanwhile, was not thinking of anything in particular. He just wanted to quickly complete the mission and return home.

They stopped the car in front of a large rusty gate. The music building looked even more ghostly at night. There wasn't a soul around and screeching nocturnal animals made the place even darker and gloomier.

James and Tobia climbed over the gate and entered the building through an open window. They found themselves in a dark room. The light from their flashlights struggled to cut through the molasses-like darkness. On a dusty shelf were some golden vinyl records, while on the wall hung a portrait of a rather heavyset person, with a crown on his head and microphone in his hands. They walked down a hallway and into a large room with a glass atrium through which the moonlight shone, illuminating a jungle of climbing plants. Without thinking too much about it, they ran up a flight of stairs until they reached a large metal door, from which hung a broken chain with a large padlock that bore the symbol of a triangle enclosed in a circle, with two crossed swords inside it and the letters "M" and "C." James opened the door. His eyes went wide with disbelief. Before him were skeletons in blue jumpsuits sitting on old rusty chairs. Tobia shifted the flashlight onto one of them. The darkness in the room seemed to resist all light, until he saw a shocking detail: on one of the suits there was a small patch embroidered with the name "Mike."

All members of the Resistance used to use fictitious names to avoid being detected and killed by the men from the pharmaceutical company. Mike was the name chosen by Virgil, the founder of the Resistance and William's father.

"These are the remains of William's dad, the founder of Emosemvi!" old Tobia exclaimed, wiping away his tears.

James knelt on the ground as if all his strength had suddenly left him. Memories rushed through Tobia's mind; many episodes of his past life rose to the surface. He thought about when he began to collaborate with the Resistance, how he became its courier. He had transported the Reversing and other materials many times, hiding them under the straw of his cart, pulled by his mare, Berta. He was grateful to Virgil for having changed his life by injecting him with the Reversing and helping him recover his emotions. Then, suddenly, the memory of his wife Marta and his son, who were both killed by the men from the pharmaceutical company, materialized in his mind, making him waver for a moment, until he had to cover his face with his hands, sobbing. James respected his friend and gave him the time he needed to let it out.

A few minutes later, Tobia spoke. "They must have moved the skeletons. William told me he found his father's remains downstairs, maybe someone tried to hide them here for some reason, maybe the men from the pharmaceutical company themselves."

"Why would they do that?"

"Maybe because they suspected William would return to give his father's remains a proper burial and they wanted to hide the evidence. I don't know and maybe we'll never know. Now we need to move on."

The two went downstairs and down another corridor that led, via a series of rooms, to the administrative offices, inside which there were still computers on the desks and books on the shelves. At the end of the corridor was a half-open door. A light and a buzzing sound came from within.

The two companions approached in silence, peeking inside the room, in which seven men were arranging objects inside wooden crates. One of them said, "When we've finished working here, we'll ask the boss to send us the latest load from Africa. Soon balance in the world will be restored."

Due to the poor lighting in the room, Tobia and James could not accurately discern what the men were arranging inside the crates, however it looked like pinecone shaped objects. The two letters "M" and "C" were branded on the crates, almost as a kind of warning to intimidate the curious.

Suddenly a hissing sound filled the air and the men in the room froze, while glancing over at the front door. Tobia quickly looked down and realized that he had just passed through a thin red laser beam, connected to an alarm sensor. The MC men began yelling and brandished their weapons. James and Tobia ran off, the bullets whistling past them, hitting the walls, producing a high-pitched zinging sound and shattering the plaster; Tobia lagged behind, he was too slow, he had a hard time running fast because of his age. James realized this out of the corner of his eye. Soon their pursuers would catch up and Tobia would be the first to die.

James, without thinking twice, stopped in front of a double door that Tobia had just passed through.

"James, come on! Don't stop!" Tobia exclaimed, looking back at his companion.

In the meantime, the bullets continued to hiss through the air, as if they were the heralds of Death announcing its arrival. James was an ordinary man and not particularly courageous. He hadn't taken many risks in life, and often feared even his own shadow, but the human mind is equipped with a mechanism that can suddenly induce an ordinary man to perform extraordinary deeds. This was exactly what happened.

"We will never make it! The Resistance has to know what we discovered here! For William, for Emosemvi, for freedom!" James shouted, drawing his pistol from his holster and quickly locking the double doors, leaving Tobia on the side of safety. Gunshots were heard, James fell to the ground, taking his last breath inside that dark and decrepit building.

Tobia took two steps forward towards the door, as if he still harbored the hope of saving his friend, but he put aside his instincts and, regaining a sense of rationality, he ran towards the exit. Once he reached the car, he sped off, disappearing into the darkness of night, its silence broken only by the roar of the engine and his sobs.

3. Never Odd or Even

Meanwhile, William, Romance and Medea, unaware of what had happened to Tobia and James, made their way towards the National Central Library of Rome, along the Muro Torto road. This ancient street is an architectural marvel that consists of a high Roman wall, which was later incorporated into the Aurelian Wall.

"Rome truly is a monument to history," thought William as he recalled how he had given a lecture at the university about that famous wall, which was built by Emperor Aurelian to defend the city from barbarian attacks.

When they arrived at the library they were greeted by the librarian. He was a thin man with thick, round glasses; his well-combed hair, parted on one side, gave him a look of elegance, and made him appear even younger than he really was.

"We're looking for a rare book," William said, turning to the young man.

"I can definitely help you. What is the title of the volume?"

At that moment Romance sneezed. "Damn allergies. Or maybe I'm just allergic to books and learning."

Medea laughed a little. The young man glanced at her in surprise, revealing a look that left little room for interpretation. He picked up the handset of his phone and dialed a number on the keypad.

"No need to rush to call for help…" Romance said, snatching the handset out of his hand and placing it back in the cradle. "Can you just get us the book we need?"

"I was calling the doctor. Your friend seems not to be very well." The young man hadn't ever seeing anyone laugh, as far as he remembered, and Medea's expression had seemed so strange that he thought she was having health problems.

"We need a text from 1806 written by Francesco Girolamo Cancellieri. I don't remember the title very well, but Villa Palombara is in it," William said in a low voice.

"Let me check on the computer," the man said, turning to walk away. Romance stopped him.

"Use this computer," he said, pointing to a terminal on the desk next to him. He was worried that the clerk would walk away and alert the police or officers. The risk was high.

"I was just going to go into the other room to use the new computer. This one sometimes doesn't work. I'll give it a try though."

After consulting the library's computer archive, the young man sent the request by typing the code "1671685" on the keyboard. "They'll bring me the volume shortly. In the meantime, you have to fill out this form with your details. The reading room is on the right. Please be quiet so as not to disturb the other readers."

Once they had filled out the form with false names and details, they thanked the young man and headed towards the reading room, noticing that it was deserted, as was the rest of the library.

"Let's be quiet or we'll disturb all the scholars," Romance said sarcastically. Then, turning to Medea, he added, "Madame, if you wish, you may invite one of these scholars to dinner."

"How nice. However, I do need some time to choose the right one. I am rather difficult," she replied ironically, winking at William.

After a while, the library clerk showed up with the book requested. William thanked him and began to examine it carefully, slowly flipping through its pages, until he found what he was looking for.

"Eureka! Here it is. Look." The two friends walked over to take a closer look at the pages of the book, which bore the following Latin phrase: *Villae ianuam tranando recludens Iason obtinet locuples vellus Medeae.* 1680. The text then specified that this inscription was on display on the main door of the villa of Marquis Palombara.

"The inscription also hints at the mythological character of Medea. Your namesake," William said, turning to the woman next to him.

"Yes, I'm famous and mysterious…that's why so many people copy my name," she replied ironically.

They heard the sound of footsteps echoing through the empty library and its stacked shelves. Someone was approaching. They had to hurry. William remained focused. "The translation of this sentence may be: *By passing through the doorway of this villa, the discoverer Jason obtains the rich fleece of Medea.*"

"What does that mean?" asked Romance, preparing to draw his gun, as the sound of the footsteps was getting louder and louder.

"The meaning is that by passing through the door of this villa, the discoverer Jason, that is, the alchemist, manages to obtain the rich fleece of Medea, in other words: gold," Medea clarified, also adding, "I don't see how this constitutes a clue or allows us to go on with our search. It sounds like a saying for alchemists."

"Medea, we can't stop at the literal meaning," William pointed out. "Observe the initials of the individual words: *Villae Ianuam Tranando Recludens Iason Obtinet Locuples Vellus Medeae*. It's an acronym that forms the word *Vitriolum*. Notice how the Latin people used only the letter "V" which they sometimes pronounced "U." It's an acrostic. It's the motto of the Rosicrucians! Very interesting… This motto has a very specific meaning. How did I not think of this earlier? Each letter of the motto *Vitriolum* gives life to a complete sentence and that is: *V=visita I=interiora T=terrae R=rectificando I=invenies O=occultum L=lapidem V=veram M=medicinam*, the translation of which is: *Visit the inside of the earth* - that is, dig into the earth - *and working with righteousness you will find the hidden stone, which is the true medicine.* It refers to the philosopher's stone, an object that basically has three powers: it makes its possessor immortal, it provides knowledge of the past and future, and it gives the holder the ability to transmute metals into gold."

"You lost me at *a cross stick*. I have no idea what you're talking about," Romance said, with some embarrassment.

Medea patiently tried to summarize what William had just exposed. "It's called an *acrostic*, not *a cross stick*! An acrostic is a composition where the initial letters of a word form a sentence. So, the initials of the Latin sentence in which Jason and Medea are mentioned, form the word "Vitriolum" which in turn forms a complete sentence referring to the legendary philosopher's stone, an object that was considered magical by ancient people. You don't have to be an archeologist to understand."

"Now I get it. But what do we have to do with this stone? I don't get that," Romance added, puzzled.

William, after taking some time to think, explained. "It's called the philosopher's stone, but no one knows exactly what shape it is. It could very well be the pinecone we are looking for."

The sound of footsteps suddenly stopped. Two security guards were standing in the reading room. Maybe the man at the front desk had alerted them after noticing Medea's laughter. William and the others jumped to their feet and ran towards the exit, pursued by the two guards. As soon as they were out of the library they turned down a narrow alley and hid behind a large marble fountain. They waited for a long time. When they knew they were no longer being hunted, they returned to the hotel where the workers were replacing the glass that had shattered during the explosion. They went down the wood-paneled hall to the secret meeting room. Sitting around the large, rectangular table were Stan, Willy, Jack, Orpheus and Bringlux.

Visibly excited by the discovery they had just made, William took the floor to summarize what they had learned.

"The pinecone is the mysterious object found by the four knights in Jerusalem at the time of the first crusade. People believe it has extraordinary powers. Over the centuries it has been given many different names, including the philosopher's stone. I am a man of science and do not believe in magic powers, let alone legends, but the fact remains that this object has been worshipped over the centuries by a vast number of people. It passed from hand to hand until it reached Jerusalem; there it was taken by the mysterious knights on the four horses of different colors and hidden from the conquering crusaders. The four knights did not belong to a religious order like the Templars – they were part of a much more ancient and secret organization. After a long journey, the object reached Rome, but it was taken away from the secret organization I just mentioned and guarded by Massimiliano Savelli Palombara, Marquis of Pietraforte, who belonged to the secret order of the Rosicrucians."

"So, now you're beginning to believe the legends, too. Go on…" Bringlux said with a strange gleam in his eyes.

"I'm merely telling the story as it stands, based on actual events. Please do not interrupt me."

"As you wish. It remains to be seen why the Rosicrucians are the custodians of such a powerful object."

William nodded and paused to concentrate and get back on track. "The finding of the small golden cross near the Magic Door does not prove that the bomber dropped it. We do not know if the Rosicrucians are involved in this. I have only said that the Marquis of Pietraforte possessed the ancient pinecone for a certain amount of time. The Rosicrucians are a very ancient order. If I were to say that they were the custodians of this object for centuries I could be wrong, because nobody knows for sure. Let's proceed by looking carefully at the facts."

He reached for a glass of water from the table and hesitated for a moment before drinking, mindful of what had happened to his mother. Then he continued. "Over the centuries, the shape of the philosopher's stone has transformed and been adapted into the shape of an egg. It was described by Bacon, Thomas Aquinas, and Jung himself, who uses it as a metaphor for the process of psychic development of human beings. What I have not yet been able to focus on is the meaning of the symbol found on the bottom of the plate aboard the Elpis - a circle with a triangle inside, which in turn enclosed a square and a smaller circle. In ancient times all references to the philosopher's stone were concealed by symbols and among them is the one found on the bottom of the plate."

"The square and the circle represent the same symbol: squaring the circle!" exclaimed Medea.

William nodded, adding, "Yes, symbolically, the circle has always represented the sky and the square the earth. So, by making these two figures coincide in a geometric way is like making the spirit coincide with matter; this is the process of creation, a theme dear to religion, science, alchemists and all artists who use their ingenuity to give life to something new."

Bringlux spoke up in a skeptical tone. "So, to sum up, on the bottom of a plate you found a symbol representing the philosopher's stone, which is to say the pinecone. Where is this magical object now?"

"The secret is hidden in the Latin inscription that adorned the door of the residence of Marquis Palombara, now unfortunately non-existent because in 1800 the villa was demolished. At the National Central Library of Rome, we found the reproduction of that inscription in an ancient text. The initials of the single words form the word *Vitriolum* whose single letters, in turn, generate a Latin phrase, whose translation is: *Visit the inside of the earth - that is, dig into the earth - and working with righteousness you will find the hidden stone which is the true medicine...* So somewhere in the mansion, perhaps in the basement or carefully hidden away from the world was this object, which many define as the philosopher's stone, and which has neither the shape of an egg nor of a stone, but a pinecone."

"Why a pinecone?" asked Jack curiously.

"Over the centuries secret societies have used many symbols, such as work tools, geometric shapes or the image of eyes. The pinecone has been less used than others, precisely because they wanted to conceal it from the view of the world. Pinecones have always been associated both with eternal life, because they are the fruit of evergreen trees, and spiritual enlightenment, because its shape is suggestive of the pineal gland in the human brain, also known as "the third eye." The philosopher Descartes points to the pineal gland as the seat of the soul. In some ancient cultures, including in India, people are taught how to awaken the third eye, which has been represented in many ways throughout history. One famous example is the Egyptian eye of Ra. So, the symbol of the pinecone alludes to the awakening of consciousness and the highest degree of spiritual enlightenment. Before my mother died, she managed to say, "The pinecone in front of the emperor's eyes and in his head." Not only did she want to refer to the legend of the pinecone that was placed on the dome of the Pantheon, but by saying "in the head" she was also alluding to the pineal gland. With her final words she managed to guide me to the truth!"

As he was speaking, William noticed Orpheus's blank stare but thought it was due to fatigue, so he didn't pay too much attention to it.

Captain Willy stood up and placed the photographs taken at the Vatican of the large pinecone in the center of the table. "These are the detailed photos of the bronze sculpture."

William examined the photos and didn't notice anything unusual about it, but suddenly something caught his attention. Attached to the capital on which the large pinecone rested was a yellowed piece of paper where the following, barely-legible message could be read: *In hoc loco erat... de fidelio animarum purgatorio... Rex... hodie Romae.*

"Someone is guiding us. See? It says, *It was in this place... the souls in purgatory... King... today in Rome.* I'm not sure I translated it perfectly, my Latin is a little rusty."

Looking at the photos more carefully he noticed a groove on the top of the large pinecone. "Of course! *It was here, in this place!* The object we are looking for was stored inside the sculpture. The large pinecone in the Vatican is a casket designed in the first century AD to hold the smaller pinecone. The top part of the large sculpture, popularly called the "dome" can actually be opened. It is an eighteenth-century reconstruction screwed onto the Roman original. The small pinecone was kept there for centuries. We have no idea when it was taken to the house of the Marquis Palombara for safekeeping. *The souls in purgatory, King, today in Rome* is an enigma that's not easy to solve."

Medea spoke up. "Is there any art work in Rome dedicated to souls in purgatory?"

"None in Rome," William replied.

A moment of silence followed. And then Bringlux corrected him. "Actually, that is not correct. The Church of the Sacred Heart of Suffrage in vernacular is called the "Church of the Souls of Purgatory" because it houses a museum containing objects that meant to prove the existence of Purgatory and the souls of the dead. The Church of the Sacred Heart of Suffrage was built in the late 19th century by a missionary, but a few years after it was built, it was destroyed by fire. The flames left some traces on a pillar just behind the high altar. The missionary thought he recognized in them the features of a face with a sad expression. Then other strange figures were found on the walls of the church. The missionary was so impressed by it that he began to travel the world to see if something similar had happened elsewhere. He collected many documents and objects related to the souls of purgatory and exhibited them all in his church in Rome. Essentially, when the deceased are in purgatory, in order to purify themselves from their sins, they had to leave traces on certain objects to attract the attention of the living, so that the living would arrange masses to celebrate and remember them. This would let the deceased leave purgatory and reach heaven."

"We need to go to that church to find out what the movements of the pinecone were!" exclaimed William.

"Maybe we'll even be able to find out where it is now. It's probably still buried near the Alchemical Door."

"I'm sorry to disappoint you, but we arrived too late. The pinecone is in the hands of the MC men," Stan said, pointing to Orpheus. "When we were in the Vatican Museums in the Cortile della Pigna, a man in a fancy blue suit approached Orpheus and showed him an object in the shape of a pinecone and since then he hasn't been able to feel emotions."

Captain Willy shook his head with concern. "I knew it! That object is cursed! See what it did to Orpheus!"

William turned to Orpheus. "How are you feeling?" he asked.

"Confused."

"When we were in Africa years ago, you told me about your wife and how she had been forced to work for MC. What do you think about that?"

"That's not entirely correct."

"What emotion does it stir in you?"

"I don't know," he replied, staring blankly.

After this telling exchange with his friend, William asked Bringlux if he still had the Reversing serum to reactivate emotions. He nodded and took a vial out of the drawer of the table.

It was time to coordinate operations.

"Let's see if it works on Orpheus," William said. "Stan, Willy and Jack you will stay with him and help him recover his emotions. Inject the Reversing and within an hour have Orpheus experience the seven basic emotions: anger, fear, happiness, sadness, disgust, surprise and contempt. You should be able to see some results quickly. Gradually, all his emotions will begin to appear. His facial muscles will reawaken and he will be able to express them. If he does not feel the seven basic emotions within an hour, there's nothing we can do for him.

Tomorrow morning, Romance, Medea and I will go to the Museum of the Souls of Purgatory. Even though the pinecone ended up in the hands of MC, we must follow its path so we can get to its last known destination. Whatever we discover will bring us closer to the truth and most importantly help us understand the whereabouts of Beatrice and Virgil. My mission is to find them. Everything else can wait."

4. Live Not on Evil

That night the city of Rome was quieter than usual. Even the Tiber seemed to flow more carefully, caressing the ancient bridges gently and rushing silently, sporadically collecting the reflections of the stars, cradling them a bit, and then helping them fall back asleep, lulled by the waves.

The night passed quickly. Soon the rays of the morning sun smoothed down the rooftops of the ancient homes, snuck down alleyways and woke them up slowly. William opened the window of his room and breathed in the history-rich air without which he could not have lived: he felt at home there. The thought of having Italian ancestors made him proud.

And then his thoughts went to his wife and son. He wondered where they were and above all if they were still alive. He missed them both very much and felt helpless - he did not know how to speed up his search. Following the traces of the pinecone-shaped artifact would lead them to MC and consequently his loved ones, of this he was certain.

He went to knock on Medea's door and suggested they have a quick breakfast. They hurriedly ate a few rice cakes and then went down to the lobby. Romance was already there, waiting for them with a map of the city in his hand. As soon as he saw them, he said: "The Museum of the Souls of Purgatory is not far from here. Fifteen-minutes' walk."

They quickly left the hotel and headed down a number of alleys of the still silent city. A bitter cold urged them to pick up the pace.

Once they had crossed Umberto I Bridge, leaving behind them the Tiber river, they could see the Church of the Sacred Heart of Suffrage in the distance, its characteristic neo-Gothic facade and rose window rising above so that light could filter into the building. They entered the sacristy that housed the museum and began to observe the objects on display; among them, the most disturbing was that of a handprint on the burned pages of a sacred book. There were also many garments on which the imprint of a burnt hand could be discerned.

"Think," William mentally repeated to himself, hoping to be able to grasp even the most insignificant of clues, trying to awaken his thought process and reasoning. The place was full of unique objects, but none of them seemed to bring him closer to the truth.

Romance stood to one side, convinced that he was of no use; history had never been his forte and he feared getting in the way of the research. So, to make himself useful, he stood watch at the entrance of the museum, ready for the worst.

The exhibits were numerous. If just one of them were authentic, it would be proof of the existence of the afterlife and, in particular, of Purgatory, the place where souls waited for purification. Medea, with her inquiring green eyes, meticulously read the descriptions under the various objects. Time passed quickly; hopes of finding what they were looking for faded.

Romance, tired of being a lookout, joined his companions, wandering here and there. Suddenly he spoke up. "Ah, so even important people have souls."

"What was that, Romance?" asked Medea.

"Nothing, I was just thinking out loud."

William approached Romance and asked him to repeat what he had just said. While he felt that his friend might not be of any help in that particular moment, he did not want to embarrass him by only asking him to be the lookout, so he encouraged him to speak up.

"I don't know Italian well, but this caption seems to tell the story of a king."

"That's exactly what we're looking for! Come here, Medea! Bravo, Romance."

"For once I've helped out with historical research... so what does it mean?"

William quickly read the text in the caption and summarized it for his friends. "This coat, covered with burn marks, belonged to an Italian sentry who, in 1932, was on guard during the night at the Pantheon, where King Umberto I of Italy is buried, along with Queen Margherita and King Victor Emmanuel II. King Umberto I was assassinated in 1900 and even today the guards proudly keep watch over his tomb. The sentry said that while he was on duty at the Pantheon, the ghost of King Umberto I appeared to him and laid a fiery hand on his shoulder, entrusting him with a message for his son Victor Emmanuel III."

"A compelling story, but why should we care?" asked Romance curiously.

William paused in an attempt to regroup his ideas, then continued. "It's about the message found in the Cortile della Pigna on that yellowed piece of paper, remember? It said that it *was in this place, the souls in purgatory, King, today in Rome*. We have already interpreted the first sentence of *was in this place* to mean that the ancient artifact of the pinecone was kept for a certain amount of time in the Vatican inside the large pinecone sculpture. The two phrases: *the souls in purgatory* and *today in Rome* led us here, but I couldn't understand the significance of the word *King*. At first I thought of the King of Souls, but I was totally off: the reference was instead to King Umberto I, who is buried in the Pantheon. Once again all clues lead us there."

"Couldn't they have written the word Pantheon directly on the yellowed paper that was found in the Vatican? It would have saved us some time!" Medea said.

"No, whoever is leading us there knows what is at stake. They know that clear clues could end up in the hands of our enemies, and then it would all be over. Evidently, at some point in the past, the pinecone was moved for security reasons, although we do not know exactly when. Unquestionably, it was kept inside the great pinecone in the Vatican, then here in this museum, then in the villa of the Marquis Palombara, and also in the Pantheon."

Medea nodded. "In the caption just below the sentry's coat is the name *Vitruvius*. How is that related to the ghost of King Umberto I?"

"I don't know, maybe it was the sentry's name," said William. "Now let's go because the lives of Beatrice and Virgil are hanging by a thread."

The three of them left the museum and rushed back towards the Pantheon.

"This ancient building is so full of mysteries... what other secrets do your walls conceal?" thought William. Years ago, one of the most important moments of his life had taken place in that building, and he loved it for that reason.

As soon as they arrived there, they stopped to catch their breath. Romance splashed some water on his face at the fountain in the square, while Medea took advantage of his absence to ask William a question. "Do you like it?"

"Yes, it's an extraordinary monument."

"No, I meant do you like me flirting with you?"

It was the first time Medea had addressed him so explicitly. William felt embarrassed and didn't quite know how to answer.

"I'd rather not talk about that," he said politely, but firmly.

"Whatever, no problem, I can wait."

As soon as Romance returned, the three of them reached the colonnade. Medea was enraptured and didn't want to stop admiring it. She hesitated a little longer to take in its majesty. She always felt something deep inside when she touched a brick or column, thinking of the thousands of hands that had done the exact same thing in ages past. She liked to imagine ancient people wandering among the columns in their now outdated clothes. "Although they spoke a different language, one thing united them all: emotions. This is the common thread that unites all individuals across the centuries. Whoever stands before the Pantheon - free man or slave, poor or rich, miserly or generous - they will always feel the emotion of surprise..." Medea thought to herself in something of a reverie. Then Romance called her over to enter the building.

The only people in the Pantheon were the custodian and a tour guide, who sat in a corner, waiting for some visitors. The sunlight shone through the oculus and a vague smell of incense hung in the air. William turned to the tour guide to get some information about the extraordinary event that had happened to the sentry named Vitruvius, but he was of no use, and merely handed William some flyers with historical and architectural information about the building, together with some advertising leaflets. They were at a dead end.

Unfortunately, it wasn't always easy to solve riddles or proceed with research. The ancient monument seemed to want to keep its secrets safe and share them with no one.

After several hours spent looking at every little detail of the building, disappointed by not having discovered anything, William went back to the hotel with his two companions. Once they got upstairs, Medea invited him into her room so he could see the view of the alleys from her window; he refused, opting instead to take a shower and let his thoughts settle. He reflected on MC, the old organization that had been dismantled years before, and was now back in its worst imaginable form. The origins of MC could be dated back to the time of the crusades; in reality it wasn't ever only a multinational pharmaceutical company with offices all over the world, but an ancient organization whose aim was global domination. They had yet to find out who was at the head of it. Above all, they had to discover if the pinecone artifact really had magical powers. William was a man of science; he had difficulty in believing the latter theory. However the clues at his disposal seemed to lead to a mystical explanation and not a rational one. Then there were the Rosicrucians. He wasn't sure how they were involved in that affair, but he found it hard to believe that one of them was responsible for the hotel bombing. The Rosicrucian Order over the centuries had kept a low profile and, as far as he knew, was not made up of murderers. Could this Order be so ancient that it kept the artifact over the centuries before MC took possession of it? In that precise moment he still didn't have enough elements to answer the question. He knew he had to find Beatrice and Virgil as quickly as possible - that was his chief goal. He couldn't even explain why they had been kidnapped. Maybe someone at the top of MC was trying to take revenge for something he had accomplished in the past, when he had given human beings back their emotions and defeated the pharmaceutical company. Just then, he was reminded of the words uttered years earlier by Peter, an agent of the pharmaceutical company who, after killing a member of the Resistance named Tim in the water plant, said: "Today we are celebrating the end of the Resistance. Minedal-e Corporation is like a phoenix that always rises from its ashes, whereas the Resistance is like a movie without a plot or an audience wanting to watch it." In a prophetic way Peter had predicted the rebirth of MC and all that unfortunately had occurred as a result.

While he was absorbed in these thoughts, the sound of the phone ringing broke the silence, echoing through the room and mixing with the jumble of voices coming from the street. A mysterious and gentlemanly voice, with a strong German accent, said: "Mr. Pattern, my name is Valentino, and I would like to help you, if you would allow me to do so." The voice was soft in its tone and the man seemed to know how to modulate it very well.

"May I ask who you are and how you know my name?"

"I will answer both questions and I apologize in advance for not introducing myself as I should have. I was the one who left the message on the kitchen table in your country home on the evening your wife and child were kidnapped. Despite the best efforts of my men, it could not be prevented. I left you that message inviting you to come to the Bona Fide Hotel. I am a scholar of history and would like to recover a certain artifact. My family has had it for centuries until recently, when someone took it away. Now I shall answer your second question. You are a very famous person, known for saving the world and restoring emotions to human beings- Your fame precedes you, so you should not be surprised that I know your name."

William had many questions. However, he simply said, "Alright, how can I help you?"

"It would be more accurate to ask how I can help you. At the time of the First Crusade, my family guarded the artifact in Europe until it was brought in great secrecy to Jerusalem in the hopes it could avert an imminent war. Unfortunately, when the city was conquered, four knights stole the artifact, first hiding it and then bringing it back to Europe, with the aim of gaining power and money."

William remembered how Bringlux had told him about those events, so in a hushed voice he said, "The four knights of MC."

"Exactly. I'm pleased to hear you know the story. In Europe, my family managed to recover the object and hide it once more. But history, you know, is made of twists and turns, so one fine autumn day MC took possession of the object again. In essence, we have been fighting for centuries; we want what belongs to us, we want to continue to worship it without making any use of it. Its power is best kept hidden away from the sight of most people."

"I'll be honest with you, I don't believe in magical objects."

"This, Mr. Pattern, is a good thing, for those who do not fall under their charm cannot be ensnared by their power."

"Valentino, I am happy to leave all esoteric questions to you. I want to find my wife and child. I wish to return home with them and lead the quiet life I once had, I wish that the world could regain its emotions."

"Your destiny is written in the stars, so you will never have a quiet life. However, if you want to find your family, follow Vitruvius. You were on the right track. I'm surprised you still haven't found the solution to the puzzle. Perhaps we shall meet, but maybe not. I now take my leave and extend to you all best brotherly wishes."

The communication suddenly stopped. The stranger's formal tone and words kept ringing in his head. Was Valentino part of a secret order, or when he referred to "family," did he mean his family of origin? He had mentioned Vitruvius, but he hadn't given him any further information about the sentry guarding the Pantheon, the protagonist of that bizarre episode with the King.

Someone knocked on the door vigorously and insistently. It was Stan. He stood in the doorway with a pale face and a sad expression on his face.

"Bad news from home, unfortunately. Everyone is waiting for you in the meeting room."

5. Proportions

As soon as William reached the ground floor lobby, he noticed the sad expressions on his companions' faces. Willy was sitting in the corner with his head in his hands, Jack gazed at the floor. Orpheus was turned towards the wall, while Romance and Medea silently watched William.

A few seconds later, Stan relayed what had happened. "James and Tobia went to check out the abandoned Calicraston Ville music building, since there seemed to be some strange movement going on there. In one room men from MC were filling crates with pinecone shaped objects; one of them said he was expecting a shipment from Africa. Our two men were discovered and had to flee but there was no way out. James heroically gave himself up to slow the pursuers' advance. His sacrifice allowed Tobia to get to safety and return to Gear Jesture with this valuable information."

A single tear ran down William's face, followed by many more. As soon as he recovered from the emotion, he said,

"We must fight back and avenge James, or he will have died in vain. The men at the music building mentioned Africa. There's an MC bunker there called Tartarus, but it's in a remote place and definitely wasn't destroyed when we defeated our opponents back then. Now they're surely using it as a base of operations. What they're producing and what they're shipping around the world I don't know for sure, but we definitely need to get busy."

Orpheus looked at his companions, revealing that he could express his emotions again because his cheeks were streaked with tears.

William nodded, looking into his eyes. "Welcome back my friend, the Reversing has taken effect."

"Thankfully so."

"You seemed rather confused last time. Do you feel like talking about what happened in the Cortile della Pigna?"

"Sure. A man in a blue suit, with thick gray hair and green eyes approached me. He whispered some unintelligible words in Latin. It almost sounded like a magic formula. Then he pulled a pinecone-shaped object out of his pocket; it was similar in color to brass, but shinier. I don't remember anything else, except having a massive headache and being unable to experience emotions. It was terrible! It was as if my memory had disappeared. I could hardly even recognize all of you."

"William, does Orpheus's story convince you of the magical powers of the object?" asked Medea.

"I don't know, we still have too few elements. For now, I am guided by rationality."

"Isn't Orpheus's testimony enough?"

"I believe in science and will continue to do so until I can find an explanation for this phenomenon. If that object is indeed magical, why did the Reversing have an effect on Orpheus?"

"That doesn't mean that the object doesn't have powers," Medea replied in an annoyed tone.

"We'll see. For now, let's base our search on hard facts."

Turning to Bringlux, who had remained silent until then, William asked, "Does the name Vitruvius remind you of anything? Apparently it is the name of a sentry of the Pantheon who lived around 1930."

"Unfortunately, I can't help you with that. Vitruvius is not a common name. I can only think of the famous architect who lived during ancient Roman times," Bringlux said, adding with his usual irony, "Nice guy - even if we bickered now and then."

William didn't understand why every time that Bringlux should've been serious, he always joked around instead. But then, after a moment's reflection, and sounding like someone who has just found the solution to a puzzle, he exclaimed, "Of course! We were off the mark! Vitruvius is not the name of the King's sentry. Jack, contact the others at Gear Jesture and tell them to stay safe. Get ready because we're going to need their logistical support."

William pulled a pen out of his pocket as well as the flyers he had received from the Pantheon tour guide. Among them was one that showed a cross section of the building. Then he looked for the one advertising the

Leonardo da Vinci Museum in Rome, which showed the famous drawing of the Vitruvian Man by the great Tuscan artist and scientist. With his pen he went over the contours of the figure, pressing hard on the paper of the flyer, so much so that he was able to detach the outline of it. He then placed it over the cross-section of the Pantheon and drew over it the symbol that he had found on the bottom of the plate on the Elpis. The three images - the cross-section of the Pantheon, the Vitruvian man and the symbol representing a circle with a triangle inside – matched up perfectly.

With a deep sigh of satisfaction, he showed his work to his companions.

"The Vitruvian man is a representation of the proportions of the human body and shows how it can be inscribed within the figure of the circle and the square. The circle represents the heavens, that is, divine perfection; while the square symbolizes the earth, or the dimension of human reason. If we superimpose the symbol of the triangle found on the bottom of the plate over the drawing by Leonardo da Vinci, it matches up perfectly. Not only that, but both of them respect the outline of the cross-section of the Pantheon. The monument obeys the dictates of the famous Roman architect Vitruvius and it seems to perfectly inscribe a circle within a square. Also, guess what geometric shapes are on the floor of the building?"

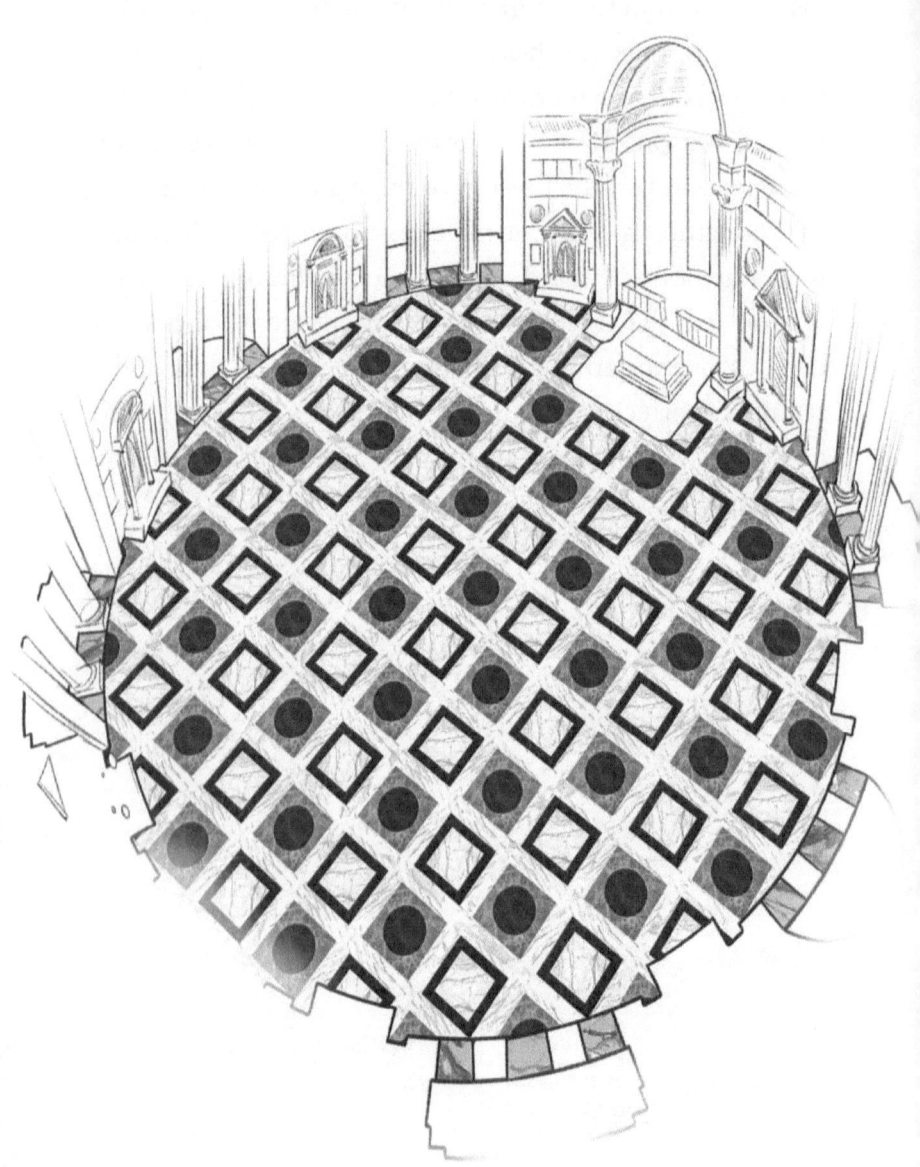

Pantheon: The polychrome marble floor with circles and squares

Medea widened her eyes in amazement. "Circles and squares! And in some cases, even circles inside squares! But of course! Vitruvius didn't build the Pantheon, but at a certain point in history the building was destroyed by fire. Whoever was in charge of the reconstruction was inspired by what Vitruvius had expressed in his famous treatise on architecture. Also, Leonardo da Vinci knew a lot about the art of proportions and his Vitruvian man is an example. But I don't understand why it fits perfectly on the cross-section of the Pantheon."

"It's clear," William replied in explanation, "that Leonardo was aware of the ancient pinecone. Through his drawing of the Vitruvian man, which coincides with the symbol of the philosopher's stone found in the bottom of my plate, he left a trail so that people could identify one of the places where it was kept."

"Why in the Pantheon, of all places? Why choose a Catholic church?" asked Orpheus.

"I don't know. In any case, before the Pantheon became a Catholic church, it was a pagan temple, and perhaps the only one to have remained intact. It is a place where architectural, mathematical and engineering rules coexist with art."

"So, Leonardo belonged to a secret order?" asked Romance.

William replied pensively, "We will never know for sure about that. But what we do know is that the pinecone artifact was kept in a variety of places over the years for security reasons, and that one of those places is the

Pantheon. Perhaps there is still a clue there that can lead us to the mysterious MC man who managed to steal the artifact."

Romance, despite trying to follow the discussion to the best of his ability, wasn't sure if he really understood how the events unfolded, so he spoke up timidly. "I don't want to ask silly questions, but I need to really understand what happened because I'm a little confused. So many things have happened. In short: for centuries the pinecone was kept safe by the Rosicrucian Order by hiding it in various places, such as in the great sculpture of the Vatican and in the Pantheon. The object was also in Jerusalem for some time, after which four knights from MC took it away and brought it back to Rome. The Rosicrucian Order managed to regain possession of the pinecone and went on to hide it in various places, including the villa of the Marquis Palombara and the Church of the Souls of Purgatory. Afterwards, MC managed to find the ancient pinecone and get possession of it again. Did I forget anything? So many twists and turns in the story... "

"Bravo Romance, you got it all right. However, we don't know for sure if the pinecone was guarded for centuries by the Rosicrucians themselves. Anyway, your knowledge of history is definitely improving: soon you'll be able to graduate," said Medea with a smile.

A pleased expression appeared on Romance's face.

Stan wanted to complete the reconstruction of the facts. "The message on the yellowed piece of paper found on the capital in the Vatican that said *was in this place, of the souls in purgatory, King, today in Rome* led you to the Museum of the Souls of Purgatory; the clues there led you to the Pantheon, where Leonardo da Vinci left us another clue to help us find the artifact."

"Exactly. The Pantheon was chosen by Leonardo because it represents perfect proportions and that is exactly what he wanted to represent in his drawing of the Vitruvian man," William replied.

Medea, sounding like someone who was about to give everyone bad news, made an announcement. "Actually, I don't know if a safe place in that ancient building even exists where the artifact could be hidden. The Pantheon doesn't have dungeons or anything like catacombs."

"That's not entirely accurate," William corrected her. "When the building was converted into a Christian church, Pope Boniface IV had many bones of Christian martyrs removed from the Roman catacombs and brought there. It took twenty-eight wagons to transport them to the Pantheon, where they were buried under the main altar. There is just enough space there to store any object and hide it from the view of the world. Just before it closes to the public, we'll go to the Pantheon. Romance and the others will take care of the custodian, while Medea and I will try and access the hidden compartment below the altar."

6. Number Sequences

As soon as the evening and its long dark fingers began to extend its grip across the alleys of the city, the members of Emosemvi left the hotel. After crossing Piazza della Rotonda, they arrived at the Pantheon. "We're closing soon, folks," the custodian warned them. William and Medea ignored him and proceeded towards the altar, while their companions invited the custodian to sit down. He could feel neither fear nor anger, so after stammering something, he obeyed.

Once they reached the main altar, they looked around and found exactly what they were seeking. The marble slab on the floor was square in shape, and carved within it was a circle.

"Of course, the Vitruvian man inscribed in a circle and a square," thought William. With a firm hand he took a nearby stanchion, stuck it into a hoop embedded in the marble, and leaned on it for leverage. Medea helped him press down on it until the slab was raised, emitting a dry scraping sound that echoed through the empty building. A steep staircase led down into the dark crypt. William lit a lighter and began his descent. Medea, visibly excited, followed him without hesitation. The crypt was small and full of bones covered with cobwebs; a strong smell of mold and rotten wood made the air almost unbreathable. They lit the wick of an oil lamp attached to a wooden beam, whose dancing flame made the place even more spectral. In a small recess in the wall was a wooden chest with the symbol of a pelican engraved on the top. In its beak was a cross with a red rose; just below there were two small combination rollers engraved with numbers. The right numerical sequence was necessary to open the chest. Beneath it was a message in Latin written on a piece of yellowed parchment paper that was covered in dust: *numera stellas, si potes.*

"It means *count the stars, if you can,*" William said. "To find the combination you have to look at the stars, but how can someone count them all?"

"Why don't we force open the chest? What's the point of finding the combination?" Medea asked.

"We can't force it because it would risk ruining whatever is inside. We can't be sure that there's not a mechanism inside that would destroy its contents. We have to act carefully."

"Could it have something to do with the stars that can be seen through the opening at the top of the dome?" asked Medea.

"I don't think so. I can't think of anything."

"We could come back at night and observe the heavenly vault through the oculus..."

"Right! Of course! I should have thought of it... once again, you've given me a hint. Repeat what you said."

"We should come back at night and observe the heavenly vault..."

"That's it: the solution is not in the vault of the skies, but in the vault of the Pantheon. We don't need to count all the stars, only the ones on the coffers of the building!"

William pulled out the flyer he had received earlier from the tour guide. After carefully examining it for a few moments, he said, "The vault of this building consists of twenty-eight square coffers. Twenty-eight was considered the perfect number in antiquity, along with the number seven. In fact, if we add the seven numbers "1+2+3+4+5+6+7" we get twenty-eight. The combination to open the casket is composed of the number 2 and the number 8."

Pantheon: vault with five rows of 28 coffers

He turned the combination rollers until the two numbers appeared on the same axis, at which point a mechanism emitted a metallic sound and triggered the release of the upper part of the chest. As soon as they raised it up, they saw a hollow space covered with white and light blue velvet with a rose petal inside, now consumed by time.

"We're at the end of the line. Apparently, the pinecone was kept here. I may be skilled with riddles and Latin inscriptions, but we definitely do not have sufficient evidence to understand where this single rose petal is leading us," William said grimly.

The two of them left the crypt and replaced the marble slab. Unfortunately, at the exit they did not find their companions from Emosemvi but two police officers. Without saying a word, they handcuffed William and Medea and led them to a black van parked right in the middle of Piazza della Rotonda, next to the fountain. Medea and William did not resist arrest because they knew they had committed a crime by preventing the closing of the Pantheon and entering the crypt. An officer pushed them into the back of the van, then got into the front seat next to the driver and the vehicle sped off.

William thought of his Emosemvi comrades. "Where could have they taken them? Have they been killed yet?" A moment before he climbed into the van, he noticed something unusual, so he said in a soft voice, "One of the officers frowned when he handcuffed me."

"So?" asked Medea.

"It's a typical expression of anger. Since the city's inhabitants no longer have emotions, it seems highly suspect. I don't think these are real policemen; these are MC agents!"

"Are they going to kill us?"

"No, they would've done it already. I don't know what they want from us, but hopefully they'll be able to lead us to Beatrice and Virgil."

Medea turned away with a huff of anger.

The rear compartment of the van had no windows, so no light filtered inside. Medea, despite having her hands tied behind her back, managed to reach for William's hands. She squeezed him tightly. Neither of them knew what was going to happen next. In their hearts they felt a mixture of both deep sadness and fear.

After several miles the vehicle halted abruptly. The agents opened the rear door and put hoods over the prisoners' heads, then led them into a room and sat them down on two chairs. Once the handcuffs were removed, their wrists were secured to the backs of the chairs with a rope. They then walked out, slamming the door. Judging by the silence of the place and the howling dogs, they assumed they were in the countryside. The ground beneath their feet was quite soft so William deduced that they were inside a barn. "It must be a farm where the animals are slaughtered: there's the strong acrid smell of the substance they use to wash the floor after slaughtering," he thought. A flash of light filtered through the black fabric of their hoods; thunder rattled the window panes. After a short time, rain came pouring down, covering the world with its liquid mantle and plunging it into darkness. The rainwater made its way through the cracks in the roof of that building and dripped on them, forming puddles that splashed up on the metal chairs to which the two prisoners were tied.

After a while, the door opened. Footsteps were heard and a bright light illuminated the room.

"Good heavens, I ordered you to treat them better, especially her!" a man said, addressing his staff. "William, I am a gentleman. I never wanted to go this far. I do things big, I move financial capital, I plan every move, but kidnapping people is not my style. But this time you forced me to do it, you left me no choice. I want to reassure you: your wife and son are fine... for now."

"Who are you and what do you want from me?"

"First of all, I'd like to compliment you. I've been whatching you from afar and see you have a knack for solving puzzles. Also, although you studied psychology, you show that you also know art and history very well. I am the head of MC and always have been. In the past, though with different goals, you and I both tried to save the world. I heard of your mother's death - I knew her, of course. She had a fascinating mind. I also remember your father, Virgil, a man as talented as he was stubborn."

Through a slit at the base of the black hood, and in the reflection of a puddle at the foot of the chair, William saw that the man was wearing a blue suit.

"Where are my wife and son now?" William yelled, filled with rage.

"Let's not waste time and get straight to the point. I need to retrieve something. When I do, I'll give you back your family and you can live out your dream life in the countryside. When your father left MC, he and a team of experts developed an antidote capable of cancelling the effects of Em 0, which as you know is the serum capable of eliminating emotions. He then created the antidote called Reversing and founded Emosemvi, becoming its leader. In the meantime, we at MC created missile stations loaded with Em 0 in order to spread it in the shortest possible time across earth, but that criminal of your father managed to get hold of the launch codes. Only two other people besides him knew the codes and unfortunately they died. One was named Paul Shelton Malthen, the other was his son, David, who you savagely killed. As you might have guessed I need those codes and you have to give them to me."

"My father is long dead and I never heard of any codes. If you give me my family back I will try and cooperate."

"Maybe you don't understand who you're dealing with!"

The man ordered Medea's wrists to be released and her hood removed. The woman screamed and barely managed to say, "It's you! I'll..." before a gunshot was heard, which was followed by a thud as Medea's body fell to the ground.

"No! You murderer!" cried William trying to free himself from the ropes, but they seemed to tighten more and more with each of his movements.

"Now perhaps you will be more reasonable. I set the terms. You have one week to bring me the codes. I'll contact you and let you know the meeting place."

A sleeping gas was sprayed into William's face through the fabric of the hood and in an instant the world began to spin around him until he lost consciousness.

When he awoke he was lying on the bed in his room in the Bona Fide Hotel. He sat up, thinking he had had a nightmare, but after rolling up the sleeve of his coat, he noticed the rope marks around his wrists. He also had a headache. He had no idea who or what had brought him to the hotel. Medea had been murdered. Beatrice and Virgil's lives were at risk, he didn't have the codes, and all seemed to be lost. His father had been dead for a long time. In fact, William had never personally met him; the only memory of him was from years earlier when he went into an abandoned movie theatre called Eversten. He had watched a video projection there, where his father had revealed important details about the organization of the Resistance.

William knew that he could not report the disappearance of his Emosemvi comrades or his family to the police, because MC had spies everywhere. It was just too risky.

While these thoughts milled through his mind, the phone rang.

"Mr. Pattern, this is Valentino. I would like to once again provide you with my help if you will allow me. I am sorry for your family, Medea, and the other members of Emosemvi."

"How do you know what happened? Where is my family?"

"The history of mankind is full of questions which we still struggle to answer, Mr. Pattern."

"This is no time for sound bites and slogans. I'm fed up with all these mysteries! I need help now."

After sighing deeply, the man said, "All right Mr. Pattern, I'll meet you in two hours at the Janiculum. Every day at noon a cannon fires a blank shot there. It won't be hard for you to find."

The conversation ended. William put the receiver back and let his gaze wander around the room. He couldn't trust the man dressed in blue. Maybe his companions had already been executed, as well as Beatrice and little Virgil. Did Valentino really want to help him? Or was he setting a trap? Even the story of the missiles was absurd. What had happened up until that moment seemed more like a revenge by MC against him, personally. It was as if someone wanted to make him pay. His thoughts went to Medea; sadness came over his heart. She had been valuable and although he had not known her for a long time, he would miss her.

To contain and manage his growing anger, William did several sets of push-ups, trying to free his mind. Exercise was an outlet, it helped him focus and maintain muscle tone. In the future, he would need both his muscles and his brain to deal with the enemy.

7. A River of Emotions

As soon as he walked into the hotel lobby, William grabbed a map of the city. Bringlux stood behind the reception desk talking to a customer. The two exchanged a quick glance, there was sadness in the hotel owner's eyes.

"Perhaps in addition to knowing about the kidnapping of my companions he also knows about Medea's death," thought William. Outside the hotel, the police patrol car had left, thinking probably that there would be no further risk of attack.

William walked out of the Bona Fide and towards the Janiculum Hill. The sky was clear, the crisp air crept into the folds of the coats of the passers-by, convincing them to walk faster toward their destination. The alleys of the city were plunged into silence and although the stores were open, none of the owners stood at their front doors as they used to do, inviting tourists in to see their wares. Such a historically rich city, a city that had survived wars and plundering, seemed to be waiting sadly as the grip of silence tightened around it, crushing it, taking its breath away.

When he reached the Tiber River, he took the bridge next to the Tiber Island. He recalled having read something in the past about the brotherhood of the Sacconi Rossi, a sect that was founded in the 17th century, whose headquarters were located there. The members of this confraternity wore a characteristic hooded robe with a red cloak; their task was recovering and burying people who drowned in the Tiber and whose bodies remained unclaimed. Each road and alleyway had its own fascinating story, just waiting for those interested in hearing it.

After about twenty minutes of walking, he saw the Janiculum in the distance, but next to the balustrade above the cannon, there was no one there. He began to walk back and forth nervously. "Maybe Valentino was discovered and killed," he thought. Unfortunately, since MC had risen from the ashes, no human being was safe anymore, people lived in constant fear and uncertainty.

After waiting for about an hour he decided to go back to the hotel. With a sad look and his head full of thoughts he started his descent. Taking the same road back, he reached the bridge at Tiber Island and heard someone say his name. He turned around and saw a man with gray hair and eyes as black as coal approaching with a slow step. He seemed to have appeared out of nowhere and it took him by surprise. He was wearing a beige coat over an elegant suit of the same color, a yellow shirt and a red tie. His style was somewhat extravagant. His features looked ruddy, mountainous, and craggy. They were sharp, but at the same time harmonious. Generally, when meeting someone for the first time, William sought to latch onto the smallest detail so that he could form an idea of the person in front of him. Such an act was impossible with this man; his pitch-black eyes revealed nothing, and the gaze looked like a guardian tirelessly watching over an inscrutable past.

"Mr. Pattern. We finally meet. I'm sorry if I made you wait, but these days one is never too cautious," Valentino said, glancing briefly at William, then turning his gaze towards the river that flowed placidly below them.

"I need to find my family and quickly!"

"Certainly. All in good time."

"Valentino, I don't have much time. I need your help. I would also like to know if you are a member of the Rosicrucian Order."

"Mr. Pattern, as you rightly said there's not much time. So, let's not waste it by asking questions that are of little use to us now. I would like to regain possession of the pinecone and you want your family back. If we work together, everyone will get what they want."

"I see. Can you at least tell me if a member of the Rosicrucian Order carried out the attack on the Bona Fide? A comrade of mine followed the bomber to a door covered with symbols in Piazza Vittorio Emanuele II, then lost track of him. On the ground near the door, he found a small golden cross with a red rose in the center."

"It is possible that a cross with a red rose in the center was located near the Alchemical Door, but no

Rosicrucians were involved in the attack. The Rosicrucians do not kill."

A moment of silence followed as two tourists crossed the bridge in front of them. One of the men, with Asian eyes, turned to Valentino and asked him in English where the Janiculum was. Valentino replied in perfect Japanese. William realized that he was dealing with a highly educated person, someone who was able to speak several languages and this impressed him greatly. Just then, the wind mustered up all its strength and blew furiously, causing William's coat to wave and flutter up behind him, revealing the red satin lining and the strong lines of his muscular physique.

As soon as the tourists had disappeared, William turned to Valentino. "Where can I find the missile codes? My father must have hidden them somewhere."

"Yes, your father, Virgil, had them in his possession, but you have not been told the whole truth. The codes are not for launching any missiles."

"I never mentioned my father's name; how do you know it?"

"I knew your father well, but we are not here today to reminisce. Memories are like the flowing waters of this river." The man pointed to the water below and then continued. "You see, everything flows. Human beings often try to cling to history to counteract the inevitable flow of time. But let's get to the point. The codes are not for launching missiles, but rather a numerical sequence for activating the ancient pinecone. It is actually composed of several moving cylinders and by finding the right sequence, which is to say that by rotating them in the correct way, its power can be released."

"A mysterious man at the Vatican Museum showed the pinecone to one of my collaborators and as a result of this event he lost the ability to experience emotions. I think MC is already in possession of the codes," William said.

"If that were true, why would he have asked you to find them? Think about it. They don't have them: I guarantee you that. I can't explain what happened to your partner. However, neither Dr. Paul Shelton Malthen nor his son, David, possessed the codes. They have been jealously guarded by my family since the dawn of time. I will tell you where to find your wife and son, but if you recover the pinecone you have to return it to me. It sounds like a fair trade. Also, if you ever manage to find the codes, which were carefully preserved by your father, please destroy them."

"I accept your offer. I will do anything to save my family."

"Good. Your wife and son were taken prisoner and brought to Rome, but then they were transferred to an underground MC location not far from Disgust City."

"I can guess where: the place where Dr. David Shelton Malthen died. The Minedal-e Corporation headquarters in Disgust City was set on fire and all its laboratories around the world were converted into Reversing production centers."

Just then, a pelican perched on the balustrade of the bridge, tried to resist the wind with its wings and flew off.

Valentino replied. "That is correct, although only the surface structures were destroyed. That location is an exact copy of the Tartarus bunker, so it extends underground. Until now, no one has found a way to access it, except the men from MC, who were never really defeated. They found refuge there, plotted their return, and reorganized themselves."

"I will leave to go there immediately," William said, his voice verging on hopeful.

"As I told you on the phone, it was I who left the message on the kitchen table of your country home, and suggested you travel to Rome. I then left various clues scattered around the city with the hope that you would be able to find the pinecone. Unfortunately, the men from MC arrived before you did. Don't disappoint me this time. I now take my leave and extend to you all best brotherly wishes."

William didn't even have time to reply. As soon as he turned his eyes towards the man he'd been talking to, he seemed to have disappeared into thin air.

He walked quickly back towards the hotel. The red banners on the façade seemed even more agitated than usual. They fluttered furiously, dancing on the forceful wind.

Bringlux came forward and told him in a concise manner that he had foiled another attack; this time the assassin had not succeeded in detonating the bomb. The hotel owner had grabbed him by the neck and dragged him into a room to conduct an interrogation, after which he managed to discover that he had been sent by MC. He also learned that the Emosemvi men captured at the Pantheon were being held captive in the hold of a ship called "Argo," which was docked at the port of Civitavecchia, not far from Elpis.

"How did you get all this information? MC men are notorious for not revealing their secrets even under torture," William said in amazement.

"Sometimes I know how to be convincing," replied Bringlux, visibly pleased. "Unfortunately, I cannot help you free your comrades and my task ends here."

After thanking him, William went to his room, stopping just long enough to load his gun and pack his suitcase. Back in the lobby, he said goodbye to Bringlux, who gave him a small black bag with five vials of Reversing and the same number of syringes.

"This serum has now become hard to find. It seems to have disappeared from circulation," Bringlux said. "The man outside has an expressionless look on his face, maybe you can help him."

Valerio, the Rotaon Ltd employee on duty at the Italian port, had been contacted by Bringlux and was already outside the hotel. He would accompany William to the port.

"Bringlux, thank you very much for helping Emosemvi once again."

"Rest assured, in helping you I have helped myself. When emotions return to inhabit the souls of human beings, everyone will finally be able to choose between good and evil. With the reappearance of free will, business for me will get better."

As always, Bringlux had an enigmatic way of expressing his knowledge. William just shrugged his shoulders and headed for the exit.

8. The Calm Before the Storm

As soon as Valerio saw William, he greeted him coldly, loaded the suitcase in the trunk, and took his place in the driver's seat. The car slowly extricated itself from the maze of Rome's alleys and headed towards the port.

It was William who broke the silence.

"Have you been working for Romance for a long time?"

"Yes, sir."

"Do you have children?"

"Yes, a little girl," Valerio replied laconically.

"Do you love your daughter?"

"I don't know how to reply."

"When you come home at night after work, are you happy to see her?"

"I'm confused, I don't know what you mean."

In a firm tone, William asked Valerio to pull the car over in a parking area, near an overpass.

"Along with your emotions, you have also lost your memories. But you will get them back. It happened to me, too. You just need to inject yourself with Reversing."

"I don't know what you're talking about, sir."

William showed the man the vial containing the serum.

"I'm sorry, but I'm not sure I want to inject myself with that, sir. Who knows what the side effects could be."

"Listen, I need a hand to free my companions. If you don't inject yourself with the serum you won't be able to help me."

"No, I won't."

"Tonight, you'll go home to your daughter and, as usual, she will express no joy at seeing you. When she's older, she'll probably go to college and she won't even be able to tell you how much she misses you. Her expressionless face will accompany her for the rest of her life, she'll remain impassive even when she gives birth to a child."

"I'm confused, I don't know what you're saying."

Valerio couldn't make up his mind about using Reversing, so William had to force his hand, even though he hated being rough.

"I am William Pattern, son of Virgil Pattern, the founder of Emosemvi. I have already saved the world once by bringing emotions back to people. I have looked death in the eyes. I have gone to hell and been strong enough to come back from it. I order you to inject the serum because if we don't save your boss, Romance, you'll lose your job, too!"

"Alright, I hope it doesn't hurt," the man said, turning his head away and rolling up his shirt sleeve.

"After the injection, you'll need to experience the seven basic emotions within an hour, otherwise the serum won't take effect. But trust in me and all will be well," William said as he injected him with the Reversing.

William then told Valerio to get out of the car. He hit him in the face with his fist. Valerio stepped back and touched his cheek; he frowned, his nostrils dilated and his lips tightened. With an expression of anger drawn on his face he punched William back, who didn't even try to dodge it.

"We're even now. You just experienced anger. Let's hurry, we have no time to waste."

William then told Valerio to approach the edge of the overpass and climb over the safety railing. Cars sped by and if he slipped he would have died instantly. At that moment his eyebrows drew together creating small horizontal wrinkles on his forehead, his lips extending outwards.

"I can't, I'm scared," said Valerio, grabbing the railing and climbing over to safety. After letting him experience the emotion of fear, William asked him if he had a picture of his daughter. The man pulled from his wallet a small, faded, but still visible photograph of a little girl with a tiny nose and blonde pigtails.

"Do you remember when your daughter was born? Describe that moment to me."

"I was in the delivery room. My wife was holding my hand. Then I heard the baby cry." In that moment the man felt the emotion of happiness, and a sincere smile appeared on his face.

"If your daughter were to die at the hands of the head of MC, how would you react?"

Valerio felt his chest constrict tightly, the inner corners of his eyebrows rose together, while the corners of his mouth bent downwards, giving him a sad expression. A single tear ran down his cheek. Incredulous, he touched it with the index finger of his hand. The astonishment at seeing the tear flow from his eyes induced surprise, causing him to raise his eyebrows vertically and open his mouth wide. Then, thinking about the question William had asked, he assumed the typical expression of contempt, lifting the corners of his mouth and raising his cheeks. "I'd get my revenge by making him pay!" he said gruffly.

William opened the cap of the gas tank and told Valerio to come closer. As soon as the man stepped forward he smelled a terrible odor, coughed, and raised his upper lip and wrinkled his nose. This expression of disgust caused him pain in his face.

"How are you feeling now?" asked William, looking at him fondly.

"I've just gone through some very strange sensations, but I'm fine. My memories are already starting to come back. In the past I know I used to feel emotions... let me think for a moment. Now I remember!"

"Good, let's go to the port, but we have to hurry because one of the side effects of Reversing is drowsiness. I'll drive, you rest."

When they arrived at the port, the security bar at the entrance was automatically raised for them. An optical reader recognized the license plate of the car owned by Rotaon Ltd. The guard beckoned William to enter, he waved his thanks, and they headed towards the pier where the Elpis was moored. William gave Valerio two vials of Reversing for his wife and daughter, so that he could inject them. He also suggested he go home and come back the next day at dawn, to complete an important mission. Before leaving, he took a piece of paper, quickly wrote something on it with a pencil and put it in the glove compartment of the car, winking at his companion. A moment before driving away from the pier, his eyes filling with tears, Valerio turned to William and said, "Before the world seemed black and white, but now it's as if it has regained its colors. I feel like I've been born again. Thank you, not just for me but from my family, too."

William nodded, smiled, and boarded the Elpis, greeting the same crew as on the outward voyage. He was met by Lieutenant Commander Marko, who asked where Captain Willy was. "Why is he not here with you, sir?"

"Unfortunately, I have some bad news. Medea, the sister of Ephialtes, is dead. Willy and my other companions from Emosemvi are being held prisoner on the ship Argo, which is also docked here."

Marko covered his face with his hands to hide his sadness at the news of Medea's death. Most of the crew had fallen in love with this fascinating and elusive woman. Everyone had been extremely polite with her in the hopes of winning her over, but no one had ever succeeded. To the sailors she was like a porcupine, full of quills and deadly to those who got too close.

"What should we do?" asked the Lieutenant Commander, wiping away his tears with the cuffs of his threadbare uniform.

"Tomorrow morning at dawn we will attack the Argo. I have been betrayed many times in the past and can trust no one, so I will only tell you a few details of the plan. Gather the best men of the crew, and tell them only that tomorrow we will free our companions. The plan is simple. We will board the Argo via the chain on the bow anchor. Get me a crowbar and give the crew some weapons. I assume Captain Willy has entrusted you with the keys to the armory."

The Lieutenant Commander nodded while remaining somewhat thoughtful. He had many questions but he knew he had to keep them to himself. Although he was the highest-ranking officer on board, he wanted to carry out William's orders to the letter. William was considered a hero and a worthy descendant of the legendary Virgil Pattern. If he had to, Marko would follow him to the ends of the earth.

William made his way to his cabin via the infirmary, where the ship's doctor was fiddling with some ampoules.

Acli's father was a toxicologist and her mother was an herbalist. In her spare time, she loved to dabble in the preparation of infusions and herbal teas. The infirmary was clean and tidy; shiny glass jars sat on the shelves, looking like crystal. Each of them was carefully labeled, but only an expert would be able to understand what the substances were. On one jar it said, "Broom & Lily of the Valley," while another said, "Curare." Farther down, on two jars he could read the words "Male Fern" and "Jimsonweed." Acli looked tired. Her curly hair was loosely tied in a bun at the nape of her neck with a pencil. Her lab coat, though clean, showed signs of wear at the neck and elbows; these small but significant details revealed that she was a tireless worker. As soon as she saw William she greeted him with a nod.

"We meet again."

"Yes, Acli. I have something to tell you... Unfortunately, Medea didn't make it."

Tears filled the woman's eyes, fading the brown of her irises. Feeling her strength drain out of her at the terrible news, she leaned on the back of a chair to support herself. Acli and Medea were the only women on the ship, and a strong bond had grown between them.

"I'm so sorry," William added. At that moment he couldn't find the right words to comfort her. He was also very tired and shaken. Too many things were happening all at once: Beatrice and Virgil were in danger, his Emosemvi companions might have already been executed. All of this, combined with the death of his mother, Madeline, and that of Medea, had created an emotional load that was difficult to bear. William, having nearly exhausted all his mental energy and being of no use to anyone, quietly retreated to his cabin.

Some time later, Bill, the ship's maintenance officer, knocked on his door. He was carrying a basket with dinner in it. "I'm an admirer of Emosemvi and will always be grateful to you for freeing us from slavery."

"Thank you for bringing me dinner. And what do you think of MC?"

"You don't see those dogs much around anymore, but if I were to come across one I would kill it with my own hands."

"Sometimes we use violence to solve the most complicated situations, and sometimes diplomacy is more effective. Do you know the history of the Resistance, Bill?"

"Of course. Your father, Virgil, is a legend and I admire him greatly."

Bill was a little bit awkward, a bit of a lone wolf, unaccustomed to socializing with people. Generally, he spent his time on the ship doing his duties and talking as little as possible with the rest of the crew; essentially, he was a taciturn and enigmatic type. He nodded farewell and walked off silently down the corridor.

William asked him those questions in order to catch any possible sign of a lie as it was always necessary to be on the alert, and not let his guard down.

The light of sunset with its gentle rays transformed the sea into a mirror, calming his restless movements and bringing him respite. With one last indomitable flicker of life, the sea swallowed up the final reflections of light on the surface of the water, bringing them down into its dark depths.

9. Deception

The night passed quickly, the stars in the sky watched over the sleeping port, fading reluctantly as leaving the scene meant they would miss the opportunity to watch the exceptional events that were soon to take place.

At the first light of dawn the strongest members of the crew lined up on the deck of the ship, each of them wishing to avenge the death of Medea and bring their captain back

safely. Deep in their hearts they also harbored the desire to take part in a legendary Emosemvi mission. Although the look on the faces of the sailors was proud, the glow of fear was also visible. Each one of them tried to contain their emotions so they wouldn't be overwhelmed, the way a tamer would do with a ferocious beast.

William outlined the plan in a clear voice, articulating his words carefully.

"We can't reach the Argo from the dock because we'd be seen immediately, so we'll swim out a distance and, taking advantage of the cover offered by the dock, climb aboard using the anchor chain. Do not shoot first. Return fire only if attacked. We are not murderers. People may die. If you think the mission is too risky, I understand, I am not asking you to prove anything, so if you want to stay here, please do so."

Acli stepped forward.

"I'm a doctor and refuse to kill anyone. It's unethical for me. I signed up to save people's lives. I can't possibly deprive them of their most valuable asset."

"I understand," said William. "Stay available on the ship. Anyone else?"

Mikey, after taking a deep breath from his cortisone inhaler, exclaimed, "I'm with you!"

Clark nodded and agreed, so did Karl and Jacob, the two brothers assigned to the engine room, and Bill, the maintenance man.

Just then, Valerio arrived on the bridge of the ship. He had been injected with Reversing the previous day by William and this had allowed him to recover his emotions and memories.

"This is Valerio," William said, inviting the man to step forward. "He has been working for Romance for some time and will help us accomplish our mission. Now, let's get a move on!"

Marko nodded to his men and they descended into the icy waters of the harbor. It was bright outside because of the sunlight - its rays shone through the early morning clouds which gradually dissolved into the sky because of the heat.

The Argo still had its night-lights on and looked like a sleeping giant. There was not a soul on deck, and no sound came from its big metal belly. It was as if the silence had enveloped it in its coils with such a force as to suppress even the smallest noise.

"Strange," William murmured, suspecting some kind of trap. He suddenly changed the plan and instead of heading towards the anchor chain to start the ascent, he ordered the men to get out of the water and make their way towards a tank, where barrels of fuel had been stacked in a disorderly manner. After a few minutes, gunshots and shouts were heard: someone on the Argo was shooting into the water near the anchor! How did the crew of the Argo know in advance what William and his men were planning? If he hadn't changed the plan at the last moment, they would've all died that day in the cold, salty waters of the sea.

"This is your doing, isn't it Bill?" said William turning to the maintenance man.

"I don't understand what you're saying."

"When I asked you last night what you thought of MC you licked your lips and stroked your beard in approval. My plan from the beginning was not to board the Argo ship via the chain and I spread the rumor so I could find out who the traitors were…"

Marko abruptly interjected. "I don't think you can charge a man just by his gestures. I don't know how the people at MC knew we were coming, but I can vouch for Bill."

Regardless of the Lieutenant Commander comment, William continued. "When you said you wanted to kill the men at MC, you shrugged your left shoulder. The lopsided shrug made it clear that you were not convinced of your claim. Then you said you admired my father, but you were betrayed by a micro-expression of anger that appeared for less than a second on your face."

The roar of shots fired into the water still echoed through the containers of the port, filling the air and making it vibrate.

"Consider yourself relieved of duty," William said, nodding to Valerio who quickly drew his narcotic pistol and injected Bill in the neck. To the amazement of those present, the man slumped to the floor in a deep sleep.

"I know MC well. They have tried to trap me with their spies too many times. They're becoming predictable, maybe they should change their strategy. Yesterday I warned Valerio, and left a message in his car on a piece of paper, in which I asked him to bring along a narcotic pistol. It wasn't hard for him to get his hands on one since he loads crates of them every day - they're narcotics destined for zoos."

"I don't know how to read body language, and much fewer facial expressions, but if we were wrong, and if Bill wasn't a traitor..." Marko said, trying to defend the crew member.

"As soon as we're done here, we'll take Bill to the Elpis and when he's recovered you can interrogate him. Now let him sleep."

The crew was disoriented because they were used to doing routine tasks and not complex missions of espionage. No one thought that Bill would betray them; the bond of brotherhood between sailors is very strong and based on mutual trust. At the moment there was no time to prove the innocence of their comrade, but they would certainly defend him as soon as they returned aboard.

William ordered Valerio to climb on the crane and place a wooden crate engraved with the logo of a well-known rum company called "Threepwood" in front of the Argo. After opening the crate with a crowbar and emptying it of its contents, the group hid inside it. Then Valerio operated the crane and deposited the crate close to the Argo, the crew of which was still busy hunting for possible intruders near the bow anchor.

After about twenty minutes some shouts were heard coming from the ship. From what they could understand, because the sailors spoke with a strong accent, they seemed to be discussing whether or not to load the crate on board. Some of them suggested they leave it alone as the cargo was not destined for the Argo; others wanted to load the rum on the ship. After a while, the crate, inside which Valerio had also managed to hide, was hoisted on board: William and his men were ready for anything! A deep voice came from the main deck of the Argo. In an authoritative and peremptory tone, the man ordered the crew to put the crate in the hold and await instructions from the captain.

"You shouldn't have hoisted the crate on board. It's dangerous. Soon the rightful owners will come to claim it," said the man with the deep voice.

"What's the harm, Laocoon? After all, what's found at sea is free for the taking, no?" called out a member of the crew.

"The crate of rum wasn't found at sea, it was on the dock, you meathead!"

At that moment there was a great commotion. The wooden crate slid down a steep ramp and crashed into the hold below; it was as if a giant had just ingested its meal.

William and his companions cracked open the crate. Protected by the darkness of the hold, they walked down the corridors and began to search the ship. Luck seemed to be on their side: a short while later, Mikey opened the door to a cabin located just below deck and discovered the Emosemvi men; they appeared malnourished and wounded, as if they had been beaten for information.

When Stan saw William, he couldn't believe his eyes. He threw his arms around him and embraced him, as did Jack and Orpheus. The eyes of Captain Willy and Romance were filled with admiration for their leader, and with the hope of getting home alive. But then sudden screams abruptly interrupted their moment of jubilation. Apparently the crew of the Argo had discovered the empty crate and, realizing the deception, were hunting down the intruders. A fight began aboard the ship between the Emosemvi men and the MC men. Bullets flew everywhere, hissing and ricocheting dangerously down the metal corridors. Mikey was wounded in the shoulder, Clark managed to reach and drag him to cover, then pulled out a handkerchief and tied off the wound.

Most of the crew from the Argo was still in the hold and it took several minutes before they reached the room below deck. This gave the Emosemvi men time to begin lowering themselves into the water by the large chain of the bow anchor. Only Marko remained on the Argo to cover his comrade's retreat. "Come on!" shouted Willy, but the Lieutenant Commander, his icy blue eyes now the color of flames, could not stop firing; he was shooting to save his comrades. Changing magazines, one after the other, he fought like a lion until he ran out of ammo and was shot in the chest by a bullet. With his last ounce of energy, he pulled a pistol out of his thigh holster and fired three shots, until he was hit by another bullet. He fell to the ground with a quick glance back at the anchor chain. His companions all managed to lower themselves into the sea and, just before he died, a satisfied smile spread across his face. His heroic act gave his companions time to get to safety and swim to the Elpis.

The port authorities, alerted by the sound of gunfire, arrived quickly, and while chaos filled the port, the Elpis set sail towards the open sea, with William and the others all on board.

Marko lost his life and became a martyr of the Resistance.

"Once again, an innocent man has died because of MC. How much more blood must be shed in vain?" thought William while scanning the horizon.

Bill's cabin was searched. Charts from the Argo containing coded messages were found. In his haste to set sail, Captain Willy decided to leave him ashore, promising to contact his trusted men to have him transferred to a safe place, but once the relationship between Bill and MC was discovered, he decided to leave the traitor to his fate.

Once they were safely out to sea, the crew honored the memory of their Lieutenant Commander, Marko, with a solemn ceremony and everyone wept bitter tears thinking of his heroic act.

PART THREE

Borrow or Rob?

1. In the Footsteps of the Past

The sea was particularly rough and the sky was so dark that its reflection couldn't even be seen in the water, its dark tones stubbornly combatting with the white foam of the waves before succumbing to their glow.

The journey by ship to Contempt City lasted several days, during which time William was able to inform his companions of what had happened in Rome. He issued a new protocol to be used in case of emergency: "To activate the ancient artifact of the pinecone, you need codes that, truthfully, I don't even know. In case you are captured or in trouble, you must pretend to be in possession of the codes as a bargaining chip to save your life. Unfortunately, MC agents are ruthless. You must always try and predict the future and plan every single move. The code name of this operational protocol is "One." Giving it a name will make it easier for everyone to remember."

When Contempt City was visible from the Elpis, William suggested that the captain dock at Pier 23 instead of Pier 18. The Elpis II was not there because it was transporting cargo. Although Captain Willy did not understand the reason for this request, he agreed. The port authorities wouldn't make a fuss, because both the ships were very similar, except for their slightly different names, and because the crafts belonged to the prestigious Rotaon Ltd.

William personally thanked the entire crew of the Elpis for their loyalty. In particular, he hugged Mikey, being careful not to embrace him too tightly because he was still in pain from the wounds sustained during the action on the Argo. He then said goodbye to Valerio, who would fly home the next day and thanked him for his cooperation and for having shown courage in facing the danger at the port of Rome. He asked him only one last favor: to transport a wooden crate from Rotaon Ltd headquarters to an old abandoned bowling alley. Valerio was happy to help and although he was curious to know why he had been asked to do this, he did not ask any questions.

After getting into a Rotaon Ltd van, the members of Emosemvi were taken to Gear Jesture, where their companions were waiting for them. They embraced each other with both joy and sadness. The death of James was a terrible blow to the heart of Emosemvi. He had been a humble and great soul, living on the streets and in his old car. With his extreme sacrifice he had shown that it is not material things that make people better. And not only James had died for Emosemvi, so had Marko. Once more, MC had shed innocent blood. That night, the comrades were silent. Tired of fighting yet another battle against a powerful and seemingly invincible enemy, the thoughts of those present at Gear Jesture went to the fallen. No members of the Resistance were professional soldiers. In fact, most of them barely knew how to hold a rifle, and yet there they were, on the front lines, fighting for an ideal.

William tried to come up with a plan to share with his comrades as fast as possible.

"Friends, once again we are called on to fight. Tomorrow at dawn we will launch a violent attack on the music building in Calicraston Ville, where we think they are cloning the ancient pinecone artifact. We have no clear intel: the little information we have is what we get from Tobia."

Unbeknownst to them, their meeting was being filmed by a small camera installed in a corner of the body shop, well camouflaged inside an old ventilation duct. Perhaps it had been left there years ago by the men of MC, or perhaps someone had recently installed it. Either way, one thing was certain: at that moment MC was recording what was happening on the premises without anyone knowing.

"How can we attack the building without getting killed?" asked Tobia, waving his ear trumpet in the air.

"We'll manage," answered William. "I can't reveal all the details of the plan to you now, you all know how I feel about doing that."

"No way!" Maggie interrupted in irritation. "This time we have the right to know what's in store for us. I understand you want to proceed with caution and don't want to reveal anything for security reasons, but remember that you can trust the people who stand before you now."

A deep silence followed the woman's words. Everyone looked at each other with skepticism. No one had the courage to add a thing. On the one hand, they respected William and appreciated his acumen in planning missions, but on the other hand, they felt they needed to be made aware of what awaited them.

After a deep sigh, William agreed. "All right, I'll tell you. This is what will happen. Tomorrow morning we're going to attack the music building in Calicraston Ville, where James unfortunately met with his death. Contempt City and Disgust City were once connected by a subway line. On the day it was launched, a breakdown derailed the cars and caused the death of many people. The tangled sheets of metal were taken to an underground storage facility near Calicraston Ville to await disposal, and instead they were forgotten and left underground. The storage facility has an air duct system that's connected to the music building. We will make use of that to get in undetected."

"Will there be guards watching the building?" asked Romance, adjusting the collar of his fur-lined coat.

"Of course, but we'll have to be smarter than they are. Our goal is to get hold of the ancient pinecone; it's almost certainly hidden there."

Stan had remained silent up to that point, and though he wasn't the best person to organize an assault plan, he wanted to have his say.

"William, you know how much we trust you. In the past you have led us into the unknown and we are willing to follow you anywhere, even blindfolded if necessary. But this time the plan baffles me. I mean, I don't think we'll get out of this alive."

"As in the past, I can only tell you that each of you is free to leave. I cannot promise you that I will get you all home safely. I don't even know if I will survive... I definitely can't guarantee the safety of others."

A deep silence fell over the room, similar to the kind that settles over the world prior to an earthquake. Before the tremor everything seems to stop mid-air: the autumn leaves cling to the branches, dogs are agitated, and time stops, swallowing up all noise. Then everything trembles, and all that is precarious collapses. The members of Emosemvi felt as though they were part of a structure that was about to crumble. But they'd never confess as much to their leader. They would follow him all the way to hell, if needed.

After the meeting, the group set up beds using the mechanics' rubber work mats and settled in for the night.

At dawn two Rotaon Ltd vans came to get them at Gear Jesture. The vans then got on the highway and headed towards Calicraston Ville. As soon as they were on the highway they noticed three large cars tailing them. Thanks to the camera placed inside Gear Jesture, spies from MC knew what was going on. They had prepared a warm welcome for the Emosemvi team. The men inside the large cars planned on opening fire on the two vans and riddling them with bullets; if that wouldn't stop them, an armored car would intercept them at the entrance to the underground depot, the ventilation system of which had been filled with explosives. This time Emosemvi was in trouble; it looked like they were heading towards their final moments of their glorious history.

The cars pulled up alongside the two Rotaon Ltd vans. A moment later the men from MC started shooting their machine guns, piercing the vehicles with bullets. The noise made by the machine guns was so deafening and violent that it sounded like a hellhole had opened up in the middle of the road and that devils were coming out of it. When the two vans stopped, the fire did not extinguish. Actually, it grew larger. The windows shattered into a thousand pieces and high flames burst out of them, first licking the engines and then enveloping both vehicles. Shortly after came two separate explosions, followed by cheering from the assailants.

Former Happiness City District Chief Richard McMillan got out of one of the large cars and approached the burning vans. "Wait, something is wrong!" he said. He noticed that both vans were empty. Their steering wheels, now melted from the intense heat, were held in place with two metal boxes with long radio antennas: the vehicles had been remotely controlled. There was no trace of the team from Emosemvi!

"He's done it again!" yelled the former district chief, hurling his machine gun at the burning pieces of metal. McMillan had been on MC's payroll for years. The police had arrested him after the riot at the Happiness City Police Headquarters. After a few years, thanks to the complicity of the corrupt men who had once more infiltrated the judicial courts, he had been released.

The members of Emosemvi trusted William blindly. Although they didn't know that they were being filmed by the camera installed in the ventilation duct of Gear Jesture, they thought that the chances of being spied on were high. So, at the end of the meeting the night before, after preparing their beds for the night with the rubber mats, they had turned off the lights. Luck was on their side. The camera in the ventilation shaft was not equipped with infrared, so it couldn't take pictures in the dark. The group, using a trapdoor under a rubber mat and passing through a semi-collapsed underground duct, exited into the street through a manhole. They climbed into two cars that had been parked in a garage not far from Gear Jesture, and reached an old abandoned bowling alley. They found the wooden crate that William had asked Valerio to transport there. Inside the crate was the material needed to install the radio and GPS equipment to remotely drive the two Rotaon Ltd vans, plus some explosives.

Romance had often transported top secret material for the government. He had some that he had been "saving up for a rainy day," as he liked to say. William, following his instincts, had predicted that the men from MC would ambush him... and he wasn't wrong. As soon as the vans were attacked, the Resistance group abandoned the remote controls in the bowling alley and made their way to the now destroyed headquarters of the Minedal-e Corporation in Disgust City. There, in an underground bunker, as Valentino had told them, Beatrice and Virgil were being held hostage. Underground, an evil man plotted against Emosemvi, his hatred for the Resistance movement burning like hot embers covered in ash.

William's ploy had worked. Emosemvi had not been annihilated, but its future was still uncertain.

2. The Illusion of Beauty

The members of the Resistance reached the headquarters of the pharmaceutical company. The glass booth that was once occupied by the security guards was empty, and climbing plants covered half of it. The various dark red buildings appeared to be abandoned, the trees and well-kept lawns that once adorned the avenues were now just a memory, everything was overgrown, as if the plants wanted to hide the place from the world. However, one faint sign of civilization was still present. You could hear the hum of the fan of the bunker's ventilation system from the inner courtyard of one of the buildings. William ordered Orpheus, Tobia, Maggie and Seamus to sabotage the ventilation system while Jack and Willy waited outside the main building to keep an eye on the area and beat a retreat if necessary.

"They want to play cat and mouse... so let's see how they manage without oxygen. They'll have about a six-hour window, after which they'll have to come out of their burrow. We'll stay in constant radio contact," William said with a hint of satisfaction at his plan. He had no idea what would happen next, nor whom he would soon meet.

William, Stan and Romance patrolled the area and entered one of the buildings. A large triangle enclosed in a circle was painted on the wall of the building, with two crossed swords inside covered with the letters "M" and "C." The plaster was crumbling and the place had a ghostly look to it. Rain had carved vertical furrows down the MC logo, causing part of the paint to drip, as if colored tears trickled down it, emphasizing the gloomy sadness of the place, once home to a respected pharmaceutical company.

The men of the Resistance walked down a long corridor, made of stained glass, all the way to a richly inlaid double door. William stopped just as he crossed the threshold. He was hit with a flashback. He remembered Dr. David Shelton Malthen, the president of the pharmaceutical company, sitting behind a large desk made of olive wood and rosewood, dressed in an elegant suit, his thick gray hair neatly combed back. His large green eyes had looked like they were harboring ancient mysteries; their glow had instilled awe in William.

"Are you okay, William?" Stan asked his friend, seeing the lost look in his eyes.

"Yes, I was just remembering an episode. I was in this room when David Shelton Malthen lost his life. He had kidnapped Beatrice and I came here to bring her home." His eyes glistened with tears as he struggled with the emotions triggered by those memories.

Inside, they found the same large bookcase, its thousand volumes neatly arranged in a row, but something in the middle two shelves seemed misaligned. Romance reached out and pulled the books towards him. They rotated on a pivot like a door.

"A secret passageway to a room, or maybe even the bunker," he thought.

The three men, brandishing their weapons, went through and turned down a dark corridor. Using a small pocket flashlight, they made their way down it, reaching a large foyer with an elevator. The lit-up button told them they had reached the entrance of the underground bunker. While they were considering whether it was prudent to take the elevator or find an alternative route, so they wouldn't be trapped like rats, powerful overhead lights came on, dazzling them.

"William Pattern: I was about to give up all hope. I sent my men to kill you. You are so very stubborn: why did you come home and try and free your family instead of looking for the codes? You will wish you had died in the Rotaon vans," a raspy voice said through an overhead speaker. It sounded just like Medea's killer. "Put down your weapons or I will kill your wife and son instantly. Please enter the elevator and take a seat, gentlemen."

Once they dropped their weapons and radios, the three men entered the elevator. The doors closed with a shrill metallic sound that would have made the boldest warrior shudder. Before beginning its descent, the elevator jerked this way and that. Then, vibrating, it was swallowed up by the dark bowels of the earth. When the doors opened, William could not believe his eyes. He felt a twinge in his heart and a shiver went up his spine.

Medea stood before him with two men, dressed all in black and fully armed, on either side.

"Surprised to see me?" she asked in her usual sensual voice. "Too bad, we could have had a good thing, you and me."

William was so surprised to see her that he couldn't muster up the words to flesh out a response. "You're dead, it can't be possible," he said to himself. "Can the pinecone bring people back to life?" he wondered in confusion.

Stan and Romance were searched and then taken to a detention cell by the men in black. William was forced to follow Medea down a hallway decorated with strange alchemical symbols. They reached a glass door that led to a room with unusual furniture. There was a desk made of a block of black stone, held up by two granite pillars. A white marble chair with Gothic lines and inlaid with gold was situated behind it. Medieval objects and small talismans dating back to Roman times hung on the walls. William had no idea who his archenemy was, but when he faced him, his heart skipped a beat. His mind filled with painful memories: it looked just like Dr. David Shelton Malthen! This was absurd; he had seen him die with his own eyes years before. Once again the thought of the pinecone's supernatural powers popped into his mind, but it vanished when the man in the blue suit and thick gray hair spoke.

"There's an expression of astonishment on your face. Am I wrong, Mr. Pattern?" said the man, peering at him with his big green eyes and gesturing for him to take a seat.

"This can't be possible."

"No, indeed it is not," said the man. "My name is Ross Shelton Malthen and I am David's twin brother."

William recalled words spoken by Romance years earlier at the port in Contempt City at the headquarters of Rotaon Ltd: "Paul Shelton Malthen had two sons, David and Ross. The brothers were always very competitive; both wanted the attention of their father, who nevertheless, showed more respect for Ross. But one day Ross disappeared, and no one ever found out what had happened to him. Some believe that he died in a car accident."

Now it all made sense. Ross, Dr. Paul's favorite son, the man who spread the serum to eliminate human emotion, was the head of the MC!

Years earlier, protesters had stormed Happiness City police headquarters to free Emosemvi members. Then-District Chief Richard McMillan had telephoned a mysterious figure to ask him how he should deal with the rioters. The mysterious man ordered that no one be spared. That ruthless person who had ordered the shooting of women with their babies in arm was Ross.

"Let's get down to business, Mr. Pattern, because time is money. I need the codes and you are the only one who can find them. Your father was a scholar of ancient languages and, like me, had a passion for, shall we say, antiques. He was a skilled puzzle maker and hid the codes somewhere… if you want to see your loved ones again you must cooperate."

William moved swiftly trying to reach his extra gun, Second Chance, secured at his ankle, but Medea got there first, disarmed him, and pointed the weapon at the back of his head. Ross remained impassive. It was as if he was certain that he would not lose his life to William that day.

"My daughter was trained well, wasn't she?"

William's eyes opened wide. Then an expression of sadness appeared on his face. Everything seemed clear to him now though more disturbing details would soon be revealed to him.

"I had my daughter infiltrate the Elpis. She was the one who stole the poison from the infirmary to administer to your mother, Madeline. She betrayed us and needed to pay!"

Although William felt rage bursting through his heart, ravaging its banks as if it were an overflowing river, he managed to control himself; his family's life was hanging by a thread and he didn't want to commit any rash acts. At that moment he remembered the scene he had witnessed on the ship. Ephialtes fired a gun in the air, then directed his weapon towards his sister, Medea, and William. She had quickly drawn her pistol from its holster and fired, striking her brother dead. Ephialtes had gathered up the last of his energy and mumbled, "Medea, tell our father that…"

Ephialtes hadn't wanted to kill William; he wanted to kill Medea. Ephialtes had understood that it was she who had poisoned Madeline.

"Medea, how could you have killed your brother?" asked William incredulously.

"He was weak and got what he deserved. We boarded the ship to spy on Emosemvi. We were certain that sooner or later you would use the Elpis. Ephialtes, however, was sentimental and for some reason he wanted to betray our family; he had become attached to the Resistance. He was influenced by the sailors and their nonsensical stories of honor, values, loyalty, and tales of their supposed savior of the world, William Pattern." After shaking her head, Medea added, "I couldn't let my cover be blown, and my father wasn't too upset by my brother's death..."

Ross interrupted his daughter and completed her sentence. "It is better to lose a son than to see him join the ranks of Emosemvi. If we hadn't kidnapped your family, you never would have left for Rome, where I put Medea on your tail. I didn't know if you had the codes or not, but when I realized that you didn't have them and that you couldn't even get them by going to all the places where the pinecone had been hidden in ancient times, I preferred to remove her from the scene by simulating her death in the house in the countryside."

Medea had been upset at being turned down by William on multiple occasions and sought revenge. "I tried to seduce you many times. I wanted to get the codes from you but you were always thinking about Beatrice. She's not half as charming as I am! Well, it's your loss…" Medea approached William and grabbed his face with her hands and kissed him on the lips with force. He immediately drew back, surprised by her gesture.

"Medea, control yourself, and sit down!" admonished Ross.

Clenching his teeth, once again trying to control his anger, William asked, "Ross, what do you need the pinecone for?"

"The pinecone is the mystical object that is desired by one and all. It has been protected for centuries by the Rosicrucians." He then pulled a golden key out of his pocket and inserted it inside a barely visible slot in the center of the large stone desk, from which a small secret drawer slowly emerged. Ross took an object out of it that fit squarely in his palm. It was the color of brass, but shinier, and was shaped like a pinecone.

"This ancient object has been feared, revered and hated over the centuries, often all at the same time. Do you believe in the value of symbols and magic, Mr. Pattern?"

"I believe in science," William replied with contempt.

"You are making a grave mistake. Anyway, will you retrieve the codes to activate the ancient pinecone?"

"Absolutely not. I will not help you carry out your despicable plans."

"Fine! I'll find the codes on my own. Today the history of Emosemvi, your life, the life of your wife and son will all come to an end. In some ways I am as sentimental as my brother, so before I kill you I will give you the gift of the last piece of the puzzle needed to complete the mosaic. Thanks to my scientific knowledge, I have been able to develop an improved version of Em 0, the serum to eliminate human emotions. While my brother, David, and your mother, Madeline, were able to create a water-soluble serum, I have managed to develop an Em 0 that has a gaseous form."

Ross placed the pinecone back in the drawer and pulled an object out of his pocket that was similar to the ancient artifact, but slightly larger.

"This is a copy of the pinecone. It contains the Em 0 gas. When I met your friend at the Vatican Museums I simply showed him this object. All I had to do was press a button to release the gas and he lost his emotions in a matter of seconds."

"So, you didn't use the magic of the ancient pinecone to take away Orpheus's emotions!"

"Why do you insist on that nonsense! You're just like your father. The ancient pinecone artifact is an object of great power. It can be used to remove emotions from people in one fell swoop and to change the world. To make it work I need the codes kept by your father! We have produced copies of the pinecone with Em 0 inside them at our Tartarus bunker in Africa; we then send them around the world and to the music building in Calicraston Ville where they are distributed to our agents. In a short amount of time, I have been able to spread Em 0 throughout cities, as its gaseous qualities allowed it to reach many people all at once. By removing useless emotions from humans, I have been able to bring order back to Earth. Soon all wars will cease, hatred will be only a memory of the past, and, as soon as I understand how to make the ancient pinecone artifact work, I will be able to take back world domination and restore it to my family, after it was violently usurped from us by the thoughtless actions of Emosemvi. We waited for you at the music building but your diversion with the remotely driven trucks was ineffective. Because here you are. And today I will kill you."

Medea approached William and tied his ankles to the chair with a rope.

Ross pushed a button on his desk and a white wall suddenly became as transparent as glass, revealing two people in an adjoining room. William felt like he was dying: Virgil and Beatrice sat facing each other on two chairs. They looked frightened. Their eyes showed deep sadness and desolation.

Ross left the room and went into Virgil and Beatrice's room. He showed them the copy of the pinecone and it released a barely visible gas in the air. The look on both their faces changed immediately: they stared emptily ahead of them.

William struggled to free himself, but he, and the chair, fell to the floor. He tried to untie the rope around his ankles, but Medea pointed the gun at him and told him to calm down. Ross came back into the room.

"I offered you a deal, but instead of giving me the codes I need, you chose to come here and free your family.

You're pathetic and inconsiderate, and now I will kill you all and find those codes. I can guarantee you that." Turning to Medea, he said, "Kill him, then go into the other room and shoot Beatrice and Virgil."

The woman pointed the gun at William's temple. The icy breath of death was now on his neck. In that instant, the heart of the leader of Emosemvi, heir to a glorious history and hero with extraordinary skills, briefly shuddered and then stopped.

Silence descended over the room, covering everything with its light mantle and enveloping the soul of the man to carry him to the afterlife. No one could say if the angels of heaven or hell would claim his soul, but considering his generous acts, we might imagine the former.

At first, Medea thought that William had simply closed his eyes, waiting to receive the coup de grace, but then she noticed the drooping of his body. Instead of pulling the trigger of the gun to execute him as her father had ordered, she approached the body, put two fingers on his jugular vein, and announced that he had suffered a cardiac arrest.

William's heart had stopped one moment before the woman pulled the trigger, mocking everyone one final time. He had bizarrely managed to deprive his enemy of the satisfaction of killing him, proving to the end that he was master of his own fate.

"He's dead, heart attack," said Medea looking at her father incredulously.

"Better that way. Now you won't get my floor dirty with his blood. Now go kill his wife and son," said Ross in an icy tone.

Medea went to the other room and pointed the gun at Beatrice's head.

Bam! The roar of a gunshot filled the air. Medea hadn't even touched the trigger and, looking back to the adjacent room, she was shocked to see her father had his arms in the air. The members of Emosemvi had him at gunpoint.

Orpheus, Tobia, Maggie and Seamus had followed the orders their leader had given them and climbed into the ventilation system of the underground structure. Their initial intent had been to sabotage it. They went all the way through it until they reached a large fan under which there was a trapdoor. After placing the explosives inside, and deftly avoiding several laser detectors, they went in search of their three partners, with whom they had long lost radio contact. Just before locating Ross's office, they had knocked out several guards and freed Stan and Romance.

Once they reached the glass door and saw Ross inside, and after seeing William on the floor with his face extremely pale, they decided to break in by firing a gun at the ceiling.

Orpheus ran over to William's side, hoping that he was just unconscious, but once he grabbed his wrist, he realized he had no heartbeat. He looked at his friends and shook his head, trying to hold back his tears. Tobia pointed the pistol at Ross and turned to Medea, who, in the meantime had come back into the room. He ordered her to drop her weapon. The woman looked confused. She didn't really expect that someone could violate the perimeter of the bunker and reach the heart of their operations, so she followed Tobia's order and dropped her gun.

Orpheus turned to Ross. "We have always had the codes to release the power of the ancient pinecone. You are far less cunning than you look." The leader of MC could not reply; he was afraid of dying. Orpheus carried William's body on his shoulders, while Maggie and Seamus went into the adjoining room and freed Virgil and Beatrice.

Romance approached Ross and his daughter. "You won't get out of here alive. You'll die from lack of oxygen. You will pay for killing William."

The group, after having tied Ross and Medea to two heavy chairs, left the room and took the elevator to the surface. Fortunately, along the way they didn't encounter any of the MC agents: many of them were still in the Calicraston Ville music building where they had been deployed to ambush Emosemvi. As soon as the members of the Resistance were safely out of the bunker, Tobia used a remote control to send a radio impulse to the explosive charges placed inside the ventilation system and a great explosion, followed by a cloud of smoke, filled the air. To make sure that MC was buried once and for all in its hiding place and to seal it shut forever, Orpheus threw a grenade into the elevator. It exploded. The oxygen would soon be exhausted in the bunker and its occupants would never be heard from again.

Using the Reversing vials given to him by Bringlux, Orpheus scrupulously followed the procedure and gave Beatrice and Virgil their emotions back.

3. Check to the Queen

The members of Emosemvi decided to spend a few days at Marleyes restaurant in Surprise City so they could regroup and plan their next move.

Once Beatrice reacquired her emotions and saw her husband's lifeless body, she was torn with grief. Maggie thoughtfully took Virgil away so that he would not witness the scene. Beatrice's tears wet William's face, which was filled with a serene expression, as if a moment before closing his eyes he had smiled bravely at death.

Romance hugged Beatrice tightly, whispering, "I can explain..."

"There's little to explain," she interrupted him through her tears, "you were supposed to protect him!"

She then moved close to William's face and whispered softly, "Together, beyond the bounds of emotions. I love you."

The following days were filled with activity. Despite the sad death of the head of Emosemvi, and the brains behind the organization, a series of unexpected events followed one after another with such speed that it would be difficult for even the most experienced narrator to describe them all.

The following day there was a sudden knock on the door of Marleyes, alarming everyone. Stan, gun in hand, went to open the door. He was surprised to see a not very tall, visibly overweight, raven-haired man standing in front of him. He didn't expect to see anyone so it took him a while to recognize the man. It was the former district chief of Happiness City, Richard McMillan, who, with his small black eyes and inquiring gaze, stood staring silently at him.

Romance came over and asked sarcastically, "Your organization has been destroyed. Are you here to beg for a job?"

"Actually, Dr. Ross and his daughter are alive and my organization still rules the world. Only fools like you could think that an underground bunker didn't have an escape route. You're so clueless! And then, this choice to come to Marleyes: excuse me for saying so, but it's entirely predictable, not worthy of a true strategist. You should honor the memory of your boss. He would never have led you here... but let's get to the point. There are snipers posted on the roofs of the buildings around here, so I suggest you don't make any bold moves. We want the codes. If you don't hand them over we're going to level the whole building and surrounding block."

Romance, having no other options, attempted to conduct negotiations.

"We don't have the codes here with us. We need a few hours to retrieve them. We will deliver them to you tomorrow, at the Gothic church in Happiness City. To avoid any nasty surprises and ensure our safety, the delivery will take place at the end of William's funeral service."

"I don't think you can afford to dictate terms," McMillan said.

"Oh, yes we can," Romance replied abruptly, interrupting him. "We have something you need, so I set the terms. We know that Ross holds the ancient pinecone. Unfortunately, when we came into the bunker, we didn't know it, otherwise we would've taken it and we wouldn't be standing here talking about it. Tomorrow morning at 11:00 Ross and Medea need to bring the pinecone to the church; we will give them the codes, but they have to activate it in front of our eyes."

"Activating the artifact in front of William will not restore his life, you fool!" exclaimed McMillan.

"You want the pinecone and we have the codes. It's your choice. But one thing: Ross and Medea must enter the church alone and unarmed," Romance concluded, forcefully closing the door. Shaking with anger, McMillan reached the car and called Ross to tell him what he had just learned. On receiving the news, the head of MC didn't get upset.

With icy calm, typical of a cold and rational person, he said, "Send our men to guard the area immediately. I want snipers on the roofs of every building around the church.

When the codes are in my hands, I will leave the church. I will not activate the pinecone inside. As soon as Medea and I are outside, our men will burst in and take care of these amateurs once and for all. Without their leader, perhaps the only one with any practical sense, they're like sheep without a shepherd."

McMillan was already savoring the taste of victory, congratulating himself for choosing the right side of the battle. "I'll soon have my job back at the police precinct and the Resistance will be just a memory," he thought as he turned the key to start his car.

When evening came, Maggie went to Beatrice and William's country house to get some clothes. Beatrice needed clean clothes and her husband's body needed to be prepared for the funeral. Maggie was very nervous because she was worried about being followed, so she hastily opened the closet and grabbed the first things she could get her hands on. Once back at Marleyes she realized that she had brought Beatrice a black dress and William a coat and a suit identical to the one he was already wearing.

The night passed quickly, and darkness swiftly beat its retreat, chased back by the first light of dawn.

In the early hours, a Rotaon Ltd van stopped in front of Marleyes. Two workers got out with a coffin that they carried on their shoulders. Shortly afterwards the coffin with William's body inside was loaded into the van, to be transported to the church. The Emosemvi group left by a back door and, for security reasons, split into small groups to reach the church of Happiness City from different directions.

And it was here that our story began:

> Inside Happiness City's Gothic church, William's body lay inside an open coffin before the altar. The expression on his face, despite its pallor, revealed a hint of amusement. Maybe he had wanted to mock death one last time, and tease it gently with a smile. He had been dressed in a long, black leather coat lined in red satin, under which he had on a damask suit with a matching black vest, embellished with a red tie. His long, brown hair had been carefully combed and lay loose around his face; his dark eyes, once bright and full of life, now rested under closed lids.

The service was drawing to a close when Ross walked into the church dressed, as always, in his blue suit with Medea wearing the same shade of black as the color of the briefcase she carried. Both of them stood quietly but felt at ease, as there were snipers stationed around the church. Moreover, several other MC agents in civilian clothes were ready to intervene in case Ross gave the signal via a microphone hidden in the fabric of his suit. After the final blessing, and after the soprano had sung Schubert's *Ave*

Maria, the priest withdrew into the sacristy, locking the door behind him.

Ross walked down the nave towards Romance. Medea followed close behind with a light step, in expectation of their victory over Emosemvi.

"As you can see I am a man of my word. Now, if you please, hand over the codes," said Ross.

Romance shook his head. "Show me the pinecone first. Then I will give you the codes."

Medea opened the briefcase. Inside a velvet recess was the ancient pinecone. Romance hesitated, so Ross urged him.

"The time for games is over. Either you hand over the codes or you'll end up like your boss."

A deep voice rumbled through the naves of the church, piercing the air like a lightning bolt thrown by a mythological hero.

"You'll have to try harder if you want to kill me, because I'm still here!" It was William.

He came up behind Medea and Ross, his coat open at the front, showing his vest that accentuated his pectoral muscles. Medea's eyes opened wide. She was confused.

"This can't be true," she said, certain she had witnessed the death of the leader of Emosemvi in the bunker. There was no rational explanation for it all. Ross came quickly to his senses and spoke into the microphone hidden in his suit lapel, ordering his men to storm the church.

"Rather predictable, I'd say!" exclaimed William, revealing a device similar to a large remote control with a long antenna on top. "This is a jammer; it's capable of jamming any radio frequency. It was hidden in a compartment of the coffin." He gestured to Stan who frisked Medea and Ross and took possession of the guns that were concealed under their clothing.

"You may be wondering how I am still alive. Well, this time I will tell you. The parents of Acli, the ship doctor, are an herbalist and a toxicologist; she knows how to prepare a non-lethal that can induce apparent death."

Medea remembered seeing some glass jars inside the infirmary containing the ingredients capable of producing such a substance. On the labels of the various jars was written their contents: Broom & Lily of the Valley, Curare, Male Fern and Jimsonweed.

Medea understood that she had been fooled. "It's true, when someone takes certain substances, it is very hard to perceive their heartbeat or notice any kind of respiratory movements even the body temperature drops."

"You've learned your lesson," William said, looking at her intently before resuming his speech. "On the trip back from Rome, I asked Acli to prepare a substance for me that could create a state of apparent death, as well as several other types of poisons to use in emergency situations. I didn't know when I might need them, but I preferred to prepare for each event in advance. If I had not ingested such a substance, I wouldn't be here today and more importantly I wouldn't have been able to hug my wife and son again. When I was in the bunker I ingested the substance by taking advantage of a moment when you were distracted. You should have handcuffed my wrists behind my back."

Everyone there looked at the leader of Emosemvi with their eyes full of admiration. Medea and Ross, however, stood with expressions of astonishment branded on their faces.

William concluded his speech, as time was short.

"You can't stay in that state for long because it can become dangerous. So, as soon as we got to Marleyes, Romance injected me with the antidote to get my vital signs back to normal. This morning I put on a little makeup to make myself look pale and, after hiding the jammer in the coffin compartment, I laid down inside it. I then suggested to my companions that they not show any emotion during the funeral service so as not to make the priest, soprano, or anyone else suspicious. This allowed us to obtain the ancient artifact, which deserves to be kept in a secret place, as it has been for centuries. In the bunker, Orpheus told you he had the codes, but in reality he was following the protocol for Operation "One." On our return from Europe, when we were still on the Elpis, I put together this protocol precisely for a situation such as this. I then ordered my men to pretend they had the codes to activate the ancient pinecone if they were under pressure. We do not actually have the codes; they are probably buried with my father. No one will ever be able to recover them."

Beatrice snatched the briefcase from Medea's hands, exclaiming, "I wish I could strangle you with my own hands!"

Medea, ignoring Beatrice's comment, turned to William. "If you kill us you will never get out of this church alive."

Stan put handcuffs on Ross and Medea and, pointing a gun at their backs, forced them through a wooden door and downstairs to the crypt. All the members of Emosemvi followed at a quick pace. Orpheus, who brought up the rear, locked and bolted the door using a solid iron bar secured to the stone wall of the church.

The precise choice of the church in which to celebrate the funeral had not been accidental: under it was an underground passage that connected the crypt to the cemetery. This kind of construction was actually quite common in ancient times, and it had practical purposes. For example, often adverse weather conditions rendered funeral processions impossible. Thanks to the underground corridor, funerals could take place under shelter. As soon as the group was out in the open air, they walked to a van parked a block away, where a driver from Rotaon Ltd was waiting for them. Once everyone was aboard, the van sped off.

William intended to spare Ross's life. It was not his style to kill someone; in fact, whenever he had had to pull the trigger of a gun in the past, it had only always been in self-defense. During the trip, Medea couldn't take her eyes off

William. She loathed him, but in a remote corner of her heart she was still fascinated by him.

"Can't we work something out?" the woman said, continuing to stare at him. "You and I, I mean."

Beatrice, who had been silent up until that moment, turned to Medea. "I recognize that you have both charm and smarts. I may be a simple restorer of antique furniture and art, and do not have your learning. I definitely don't have your stunning green eyes. However, I do have one thing you don't have that gives me a certain advantage."

"What do you have that I don't?" Medea asked, annoyed by the irony in Beatrice's voice.

"I have my husband! If you try one more time to talk to him, you're going to need a restorer to put you back together!"

"Ladies, please!" exclaimed Romance impatiently.

William was embarrassed and held his son Virgil tightly. The decision to bring the child to the church to attend the staging of the funeral had not been easy, but the experience was necessary and would shape his character and teach him how Emosemvi worked. It was a kind of baptism with fire. The precarious circumstances in which the world found itself had led William to make difficult choices; certainly, in a normal situation everything would have been different. His son would have lived a peaceful childhood, far removed from the actions of the Resistance.

4. Magic Gang

As the roar of the van filled the air, causing it to hum loudly, William thought about how it felt to hug Beatrice again at Marleyes.

Romance's attempts to tell her that William's death was only a fiction failed miserably. Her heart was full of grief, she was distraught, she even ran out of the restaurant. To rouse his boss from his apparent death, Romance had not only injected him with the substance necessary for bringing his vital signs back to normal, he had also performed a complex resuscitation procedure. When he came to, William slowly opened his eyes and looked around. He immediately asked for a glass of water. He felt extremely tired, as though he had been unconscious for days and not just a few hours.

The muscles of his legs still sore, he went out and found Beatrice sitting on a porch swing, her face buried in her hands. He tried to think of something to say to his wife, but nothing came to him, so he sat on the porch swing and took her hand in his. She instinctively pulled hers away, emitted a scream, and brought her hands to her chest. She thought she was going to faint.

"Are you a ghost?" she asked in a trembling voice.

"No, Beatrice. It was only a fictional death. It was our only option."

"You break my heart and then have the nerve to tell me this story? You could have at least left me a note or something! Why didn't Romance tell me?"

"He tried, but you didn't let him speak!"

Beatrice threw her arms around his neck, and burst into tears, holding him so tightly that for a moment he couldn't breathe. After an interminable moment, she said to him with her usual wit, although still visibly upset, "Alright, but next time before you die, let me know in advance, OK?"

Holding his wife's face with both his hands, William kissed her passionately.

"I thought it was over. But once again you beat death," Beatrice said with a smile. "When this is finished, if we don't take a little time for ourselves by going out to dinner and celebrating a bit, I really don't think you'll be able to beat death again."

Smiling and caressing her face, he asked her to tell him what had happened on the evening of the kidnapping and during her imprisonment. Beatrice suddenly grew sad.

"Five men dressed in black came into the house. I was in the kitchen. Virgil was playing in his room. After drugging us, they took us to a ship and locked us in our cabins. The food was passed to us through an opening under the door... It was terrible. After several days at sea, we arrived at the port and they took us, with hoods over our heads, to an old Roman noble palace. Judging by the coats of arms I saw, it must have belonged to a very important family. We spent day after day in a single room. I tried my best to distract Virgil. Despite the difficult situation, he was always calm. He certainly has your strength."

"I know! He is a very gifted child, with all the qualities of a good leader."

"Absolutely not! I would like to give him a normal life, please. No more fables in Latin. Your grandfather used to do that with you, but now it has to stop. I do not want him to be the head of any future organization."

"Beatrice, you cannot oppose destiny. As long as someone threatens peace on earth we have to work to maintain it and that takes sacrifice. Anyway, we'll talk about it calmly later. Now let's go back to the restaurant. It's not a good idea to stay out here."

Although she wasn't entirely convinced, she nodded. Her husband was alive and that was more important than anything else. And in that moment, he gently slipped her necklace with the heart-shaped pendant into her hands.

The two of them embraced each other tenderly, their hearts close to one another, synchronizing, marking the passing of time with love and heartbeats.

As soon as Virgil saw his father walk in, he ran to him and held him tightly, crying with joy.

"I knew it, Dad, I was sure of it! You always trick us!" he said, wiping his tears away. "Next time, though, instead of doing the trick of dying, do the one with the rabbit and the hat. I like that one better!"

"Yes, you're right I am a bit of an illusionist. I missed you so much… It won't happen again, don't worry. We'll be together forever. We just have to pretend one last time during my funeral at the church. Now you know I'm not dead… it will just be another trick."

The two hugged for a long time, while Beatrice looked on with deep emotion. The family, after going through difficult times and facing enormous difficulties, had finally come together. Their hearts were filled with the hope of being able to live a normal life together, far from any danger.

William was still immersed in these memories when the van arrived at the port of Contempt City. There was no other safe place to hide and the Elpis was certainly defendable. On board they would be able to plan their next moves so that they could bring emotions back to people and eliminate MC for good. That devastating organization always managed to find a way to go back to doing its evil actions; it was like cutting off the head of the mythological monster Hydra and seeing it grow back before their eyes.

Ross and Medea were locked up in a cabin and all the members of the Resistance went to rest. The next day at dawn they would hold a meeting to decide their next moves. Acli, the ship's doctor, was very kind with Beatrice and, in addition to giving her a clean lavender-scented nightgown, she also handed her a suitcase with some fresh clothes.

Evening came and with it, darkness. The sea was calm, the clear sky full of small, barely visible dots whose shine was so bright they seemed to sing a hymn to the peace and quiet. On the horizon, however, a red star glowed with dark omens.

William, after having put Virgil to sleep by telling him his favorite Latin fable, whose protagonists were Mercury and a sculptor, went to the bridge to talk to Romance. Suddenly a bright light illuminated the sky, then slowly flickered and went out as soon as it touched the surface of the water. Not long after, the noise from a helicopter made the glass of the bridge shake. The ship was suddenly surrounded by men from MC. Some of them stood at the dock with their guns drawn, others waited out at sea in two boats equipped with heavy .50 caliber machine guns. The helicopter hovered above the ship, cutting through the darkness with its powerful searchlight. MC troops had planned a lightning attack, with the objective of freeing Ross and Medea, taking possession of the pinecone and killing all members of the Resistance. Before the mission, they had held a briefing under the chairmanship of Richard McMillan, who distributed mug shots of the Resistance members and gave orders: no one was to remain alive. Even little Virgil had to be eliminated because he could one day be a threat. A squad of men from MC came up alongside the Elpis and placed "lightweight" explosive to cause leaks. This would prevent the ship from escaping to sea.

Meanwhile, the crew aboard the Elpis was ready to maneuver. Fear slowly filled the hearts of all the members of Emosemvi, slowly at first and then like a cavalry charging. The moment had come: a violent fight was about to begin. Richard McMillan stood on the dock with a megaphone in his hands, surrounded by smoke to conceal the MC men from view.

"You have one minute to surrender!" he thundered. "Hand over the hostages and the pinecone briefcase. If you cooperate, we will retreat!" No one from the ship responded.

William was in radio contact with his men. "Not yet!" he said.

McMillan tried to appeal to the leader of Emosemvi and his feelings, showing that he wanted to offer him the chance to surrender once again. "Pattern, let's get this over with or your son will be the first to die!"

No one responded. William's voice came over the radio.

"Not yet!"

"You asked for it!" roared McMillan. The sound of a siren filled the air, explosive charges detonated and craters appeared in the ship's hull.

"Now!" thundered McMillan.

"Now!" yelled William at that very same moment.

The MC men on the pier opened fire at the ship, covering their colleagues, who prepared to board. At the very same time, taking advantage of the noise generated by the machine gun fire and especially the fact that the men of MC were focused on the attack, a ship moored at Pier 23 set sail, pushing its engines to full speed to reach the open sea.

On his return from Europe, William had asked Captain Willy to dock the Elpis at Pier 23, so when the Elpis II returned from her voyage, she had docked at Pier 18. The two ships were identical except for their slightly different name. As soon as he arrived at the port in the van, on their way back from the Gothic Church, William had secretly instructed Romance to remove the number "II" from the name of the Elpis moored at Pier 18. Essentially, the MC men were busily attacking the Elpis II, which was empty, while the Elpis, which held all the Resistance members, headed out to sea from Pier 23.

"Start dropping the nets. They are going to be on our tails soon enough," William told the ship's captain. In the silence of the night dozens of fishing nets were lowered into the sea. The leader of Emosemvi ordered most of the weights to be removed from the nets, leaving only the buoys, so the nets would float just below the surface of the water and not sink.

When the men from MC boarded the Elpis II, they found it empty and alerted McMillan, who flew into a rage. The Elpis was quickly getting farther away from the harbor under the cover of darkness and with its lights off. As soon as the former district chief understood what was going on, he gave orders for the two boats equipped with heavy machine guns and the helicopter to pursue them quickly.

"I hate you, William Pattern!" he exclaimed in a rage, throwing his hat onto the ground and stomping on it like a spoiled child.

The two boats quickly approached the Elpis, ready to fire, when all of a sudden there was an awkward metallic noise. It grew stronger and stronger as the seconds passed. Both boats' engines stalled: the nets thrown into the sea by the Elpis had twisted around the propellers and brought the boats to a grinding halt. The helicopter, with its crew of two pilots and six heavily armed men, reached the ship and stopped and hovered above them, throwing down dozens of smoke bombs, granting the attackers the necessary cover to be able to descend on ropes to the ship, without the crew of the Elpis seeing them. The six-man commando was well-trained and conducted their operation masterfully, without making the slightest mistake. Wearing gas masks, they began to launch tear gas. The Elpis crew did not have the necessary equipment to defend themselves from the gas, so the commandos advanced through the smoke without encountering any resistance. Their opponents, due to the effect of the gas, rolled around on the ground covering their faces with their hands and moaning. The six men in tactical gear headed for the cabins. William thought of Beatrice and Virgil. With his pistol in hand, and a diving mask that he found on the bridge to cover his eyes and a wet cloth at his mouth to filter the gas as much as possible, he headed for the sleeping quarters. He found Virgil with a hood over his head standing next to Medea, who was wearing a gas mask, while Ross stood a little further back, holding the barrel of the gun to Beatrice's temple.

"The artifact, Mr. Pattern! Give me the artifact!" yelled Ross from inside his gas mask. William seemed to have lost the battle. He hadn't expected the helicopter assault; he couldn't have imagined that the attack would happen so violently and be carried out with such precision, typical of a Special Ops team.

"It's in my cabin, in the niche in the bathroom wall," he replied hesitantly. Ross nodded to one of his men who quickly entered the cabin and came out, showing the boss a briefcase with the ancient pinecone inside. Ross shot and grazed William's shoulder, then aimed at his head. Just as he was about to pull the trigger for a second time, Romance came over and opened fire with a machine gun. The shots bounced off the sheets of metal in the corridor, at which point one of the attackers launched a smoke bomb, which filled the space down to the smallest crevice. Ross, Medea and the entire MC team retreated to the helicopter while William, in pain from his shoulder injury, helped his wife to her feet, then took Virgil in his arms and headed for the bridge.

The MC team placed powerful explosive charges on the ship with the goal of sinking it and killing everyone on board instantaneously.

"I know a radio signal will detonate shortly," thought William as he stood on the bridge. There would be an explosion. The artifact was in the hands of the enemy. The Elpis would soon sink, taking the entire crew with it. At that moment William's eyes rested on the explosive with its flashing red light. He would never have enough time to defuse it so he hugged his wife and son tightly, preparing to leave the earth with them.

If he could have chosen how to die, he would've wanted it to be just that way, holding his family in his arms. Although he was strong and muscular, he would never have been able to protect his wife and son from the explosion and certain death. While William was deep in these thoughts, the helicopter rose quickly into the air. Acli, the ship's doctor, her eyes as red as hell from the tear gas, fired a flare at the helicopter, hitting the rotor. Although the helicopter was not seriously damaged, the pilot made an emergency maneuver and did so in such an abrupt manner that he lost control. Ross, thrown into the void, and clutching the briefcase with the ancient artifact, came crashing down onto the deck of the ship, dead on impact. The helicopter catapulted into the sea, exploding immediately after it hit the water.

Beatrice, watching the scene from the bridge, murmured, "Medea, this is all because you tried to take my son hostage and because you tried to sleep with my husband!"

William heard the comment, but did not respond.

Shouts of jubilation arose from the Elpis. Emosemvi had dealt another blow to the MC. Their next move would be to return the ancient pinecone artifact to Valentino and restore balance to the world.

5. Top Spot

Clark had served as a bomb disposal expert in his home country prior to boarding the Elpis, so he had no difficulty clearing the ship of explosives. Acli appeared on the bridge and was congratulated by the captain of the ship Willy, for having performed her heroic act and saving the entire crew.

William hugged her tightly. "Thank you, Acli! You acted better than any man on board; you're an extremely resourceful woman. Emosemvi respects women and celebrates their courage every day."

"You ought to be thanking me twice over: I'm glad my concoction for apparent death worked and didn't kill you: sometimes all it takes is a small mistake to really send someone to the other side."

"That's right! I owe you double!"

After taking his leave, William retired to his cabin along with Beatrice and Virgil who, despite his tender age, had been extremely calm. He had cried when Medea had put the hood over his head, but then had shown great strength of will and had managed to control himself.

"Daddy, does your shoulder hurt? It looks like you're bleeding."

"No, it's just a scratch. We can control pain, my son. I'm proud of you, you showed a lot of courage today."

Beatrice meanwhile had gone to the bathroom to get sterile gauze and disinfectant to dab her husband's wound. Virgil, pleased to have received his father's compliments, asked with eyes full of hope, "Dad, when are we going home?"

"First we have to go to Rome. It's a beautiful city, one that your grandfather loved very much. Do you feel like seeing it?"

Virgil nodded with happiness. "Dad, will you tell me one more time about grandfather?"

"Sure. He was a good man and he loved me very much."

"And did Grandmother Madeline love you, too?"

After a moment's hesitation William replied, "Yes, Grandmother loved me too, but in her own way. Now it's late and you must sleep. Think of something nice. For example, what would you like to eat in Rome?"

"A giant ice cream!" the child exclaimed.

"You'll get one for sure! And we'll spend a lot of time together, just the two of us."

"When they took me and Mom to that underground bunker, I got really scared. Actually, even in the restaurant while you were half dead, I mean, when your eyes were closed and you didn't speak, I was afraid, but I tried to be courageous, the way you taught me, and I was!"

"Bravo, my little man! You were really brave!" Holding him tightly to his chest, William stroked his forehead until the child fell asleep. After kissing Beatrice passionately, William then went to the bridge.

Romance was splashing water on his face. His eyes were still swollen from the gas.

"There's one thing I can't explain," he said, turning to William. "When we returned from Rome, you asked Captain Willy to dock at Pier 23 instead of Pier 18. Why? How did you foresee an attack from MC?"

"When you're in battle, and especially if you're outnumbered, you have to try to anticipate your opponent's every move. I didn't know when we were going to be attacked, but I imagined something like this could happen, so it seemed appropriate to try to disorient the enemy. When we got to the port in the van, I asked you to remove the number "II" from the name of the Elpis to create a diversion in case we were attacked."

"Why didn't we set sail as soon as we got to the harbor, on our way back from the church?" urged Romance.

"We had the pinecone artifact and Ross in our hands; I wanted to use the hostages to lure McMillan and take him prisoner as well. Without a leader, MC would fall like a house of cards. While we have no rigid hierarchy in Emosemvi, MC does, and this generates deep-rooted competition within its ranks. Our enemies are blinded by the desire for power and always aim to reach the highest levels of the organization. If we had taken McMillan prisoner, there would've been an all-out fight within the MC. It's the old principle of divide and rule, which was so dear to the politics of the ancient Romans. Therefore, dividing the forces of the adversary would have generated rivalry within their ranks. But then they attacked us, and I didn't expect such a deployment of forces; they took me by surprise, I admit."

Romance looked up in admiration at his leader. They all saw him as their leader, even though he wore no epaulettes. He realized that Emosemvi really could have none better.

The journey lasted several days; the crew was used to facing long crossings. Ross's body was thrown into the sea and even though the man had caused great damage to all humanity, William felt pity for him.

The one who had the most fun during the voyage was Virgil. Clark spent many hours conversing with him in Spanish, and the child picked it up quickly. In spite of his young age, he seemed to be very good at languages: his dad often spoke to him in Italian and Latin. Mikey carried Virgil around the ship on his shoulders and told him fantastic stories about pirates and galleons. Generally, sailors are thought of as people with rough manners because they spend a lot of time at sea and this hardens them, but the crew of the Elpis was composed of happy, jovial sailors.

The ship arrived at the port of Civitavecchia early in the morning. Romance immediately went to deliver the cargo documents to the Italian port authorities. Valerio, still grateful to William for having given him back his emotions with the Reversing, was waiting to take William and his family to the Bona Fide Hotel. Maggie, Seamus, Orpheus and Tobia would follow along in another car, while the rest of Emosemvi would reach the hotel later.

The weather was pleasant, neither too hot nor too cold. The clear sky overlooked the city, framing its ancient monuments, those undisputed and unique jewels, capable of giving the gift of history to those who know how to grasp their meaning.

As soon as they reached the hotel, Valerio took his leave. The leader of Emosemvi handed the case containing the ancient pinecone to Orpheus who walked into the Bona Fide with Maggie, Seamus, and Tobia. Meanwhile, William, Beatrice, and Virgil went to a bar for a large ice cream and two coffee *granitas* with whipped cream. Then they walked through Piazza della Rotonda, stopping in front of the Pantheon. William crouched down next to Virgil and pointed to the monument.

"You know, that's where your mom and I got married several years ago: she was so beautiful that day. She wore an ivory dress and a tiara. If I could go back in time, I would marry her again and again. Always show her love and respect because she is a special person and daddy promised her his heart all those years ago."

Beatrice blushed slightly, turning her face away to hide her emotion.

"Dad, I know which dress you mean! I saw it once in mom's closet. Maybe she kept it all these years because she would like to marry you again, too!" the child said naively as he enjoyed his ice cream.

After spending a little more time together, they headed back towards the Bona Fide Hotel. Orpheus returned the briefcase containing the ancient pinecone artifact to William, while Bringlux came over to greet him.

"Welcome! I'm glad you're still alive, William. Shall I have your suitcases taken to the room?"

"The large suitcase can go in the room," he said. Then, showing him the black case containing the ancient pinecone, he added, "I'll keep this one with me. It contains a very precious object."

"Ah, so you succeeded! You always amaze me. Do you want to use it to bring emotions back to the world?"

"I already have a plan for that but I can't tell you about it at the moment. What about you? Once emotions return to humans, will you stay here or return to the hotel in Surprise City?"

"I'll go where I am most needed," replied Bringlux. "A certain Mr. Valentino stopped by here a couple of times asking for you. He left this card." The man handed him a yellow card on which a phone number was noted with a red pen.

After thanking Bringlux and taking his leave, William went to his room with his family, but as soon as he closed the door behind him the phone rang. A familiar voice greeted him cordially.

"Mr. Pattern, it pleases me enormously that you are back in Rome. Shall we meet this evening at 8:00 at the usual place?" said Valentino, alluding to the bridge near the Tiber Island where they had met before.

"Yes, alright."

William wanted to add something further, but the communication was interrupted. Beatrice asked her husband if there was a problem, but he shook his head in silence.

6. The Face of History

William, Beatrice and Virgil were still in their hotel room when the little one, with a bored tone, said, "Daddy will you tell me a story?"

"Leave your father alone, he's busy now. When you see that look on his face, it means that he is absorbed with something, my son. And that means, it's time to start worrying," said Beatrice with a smile.

Virgil didn't want to give up, so he gave it one more try. "Dad, can you tell me my favorite story? The one about Mercury and the sculptor..."

Beatrice stepped in and scolded him. "Enough Virgil, now stop it."

Suddenly William sprang to his feet, exclaiming, "That's it! The codes! Of course, the fable!" He went up to his son and hugged him tightly. "Thank you, sweetheart, thank you!"

Virgil didn't understand what was going on. He looked at his mother, trying to figure out if she understood, but all he got in response was a shrug.

"Your grandfather has spoken to us from the grave! I know where to find the codes to unlock the power of the ancient artifact!"

Beatrice still didn't understand what her husband meant. Virgil, meanwhile, took advantage of the situation. "If I've been so good, will you buy me another ice cream, Dad?" His mother glared at him.

"You know how you and your grandfather have the same name, right?" The boy nodded. "He was the keeper of some important codes that are necessary to activate an ancient pinecone-shaped object. But, when he was alive, things were dangerous and he feared for his life. He couldn't tell anyone the codes. There was only one person he could trust: your great-grandfather, Walter, your grandmother Madeline's father."

"Did your father tell Walter the codes?" Beatrice asked with great curiosity.

"Not exactly. He asked my grandfather to tell me fables in Latin and the one about Mercury and the sculptor especially often."

"Daddy, that's my favorite!" said the child.

"Yes, I know. As you know, the story is about the meeting between the god Mercury and a sculptor. Mercury is a Roman god known for being very swift; in fact, he is often depicted wearing winged sandals and is considered the messenger of the Gods. So, a messenger is the protagonist of the fable… What does that make you think of, Beatrice?"

"It makes me think that there's a message hidden in the fable for you!"

"That's right. Years ago, I walked into an old abandoned movie theater called Eversten, where my father had left a video message advising me to go home and look inside the big bookcase for a book called "The Cosmos and Its Mysteries." Inside the book, in addition to illustrating how emotions, facial micro-expressions and body language work, there were illustrations of several marble busts of Roman emperors. Each one depicted a different emotion on their faces. At the time I didn't pay attention to the figures because I was focused on understanding how facial micro-expressions work, but now it all makes sense. Your grandfather's fable had a messenger as its protagonist because he wanted to send us a message! Then there's the sculptor. What does that make you think of?" William said, turning again to Beatrice.

After some thought, she replied carefully. "The sculptures of the marble busts of the Roman emperors depicted in your father's book are the key to the codes."

"Exactly, Beatrice! The clues to get the codes are hidden in the expressions of the statues' faces!"

"Perfect! So, all we need to do is go home and examine that book to find the codes."

"Not quite. We have to find the same statues that are depicted in the book here in Rome: that's how we will find the codes. Unfortunately, some of the photos in the book are not well reproduced, so it would be impossible to interpret their facial expressions."

"But how can we possibly succeed at that? There are hundreds and hundreds of statues in this city. How will we find the right ones?" observed Beatrice.

"Generally speaking, Roman sculptures tend to show subjects with neutral expressions. It will be easy to find ones that conceal the secret message because they will express strong emotions through their facial features."

William rummaged through a drawer finding a tourist flyer, but it wasn't of much use, so he called down to the front desk to talk to Bringlux.

"How can I help you, William? Would you like something to eat?" he asked.

"Not right now, thank you. Can you tell me if there is a place in Rome where there are a large number of busts of Roman emperors?"

"Ah, so you finally want to treat yourself to a tour?"

"Please, just answer the question, I don't have much time."

"Alright, let me think... Yes, there are lots of sculptures in the Hall of the Emperors at the Capitoline Museums. If I'm not mistaken, there are sixty-seven busts of Roman emperors there. We often suggest it to tourists."

"Thanks for the information, Bringlux."

Before ending the conversation, the hotel owner said something unexpected. "I know what you're looking for. It's not always a wise choice to rummage through the maze of history. Some things are best left buried; they can be dangerous."

Bringlux hung up the phone. As usual, he spoke enigmatically, but this time he was clearly advising them not to proceed further with their research and abandon the idea of finding the codes.

William, however, was very determined. He wanted to find out where his father hid the codes that could activate the pinecone. Although he never actually believed in its power, he needed to understand how it worked.

Carrying the case containing the precious artifact, William left the hotel with Beatrice and Virgil. They got into a taxi and went to the Capitoline Museums, where an emotionless custodian named Bernardo looked them up and down with his brown eyes. And yet there was something warm in his gaze. He wore a uniform with a golden coat of arms embroidered on the breast pocket with the symbol of a book and a cane. His job was to guide the few visitors through the various rooms of the museums. After showing them Room 11, where there were many things on display, and then to Room 19, which was also full of antiquities, he accompanied them to the Hall of the Emperors, and took his leave.

The busts of the emperors were arranged neatly on the shelves. Some of them, such as Trajan, Marcus Aurelius and Gallienus, had neutral expressions: not a single frown on their faces, no contracted muscles, nothing that might suggest an emotion. William approached them to observe them better. Vespasian's sculpted face was deeply enigmatic; he expressed happiness with his lips and anger with his forehead.

"This emperor is depicted in my father's book. And look, he expresses happiness and anger at the same time. That's rather odd."

Virgil pointed to Probus' face. "Dad, this one looks sad."

"Good, son. You're right. The corners of his mouth are turned down and his eyebrows converge upwards towards the center. So, he expresses sadness," said William, pleased with the skill shown by his son.

Beatrice spotted a third statue, that of Caracalla, who had a marked expression of emotion on its face. "This is anger, right, William?"

"Yes, this sculpture is also in my father's book. So, that makes 3 faces that express emotions. So, the first number in the code is 3. Three has been considered the number of knowledge and perfection since ancient times.

"Vespasian expresses happiness and anger at the same time, which is completely unnatural because they are two opposite emotions. This makes me think of a number which contains two opposites: and that's the number 7. This number is associated with the days of creation, so something positive, and that explains the expression of happiness. But 7 is also used to express something negative, the 7 deadly sins described in the Divine Comedy by Dante Alighieri. In fact, Purgatory is divided into 7 chapters, in which the 7 deadly sins are expiated.

"But let's move on to the other sculpture. Look at Probus: he expresses sadness with his mouth, his converging eyebrows and his forehead, which shows horizontal wrinkles. If we think about basic emotions, where does sadness fit in?"

Beatrice thought for a moment and said, "Between anger and happiness."

"Exactly. So, this one stands between two opposites. Without a doubt the number it represents is 10, because it is made up of two opposite numbers, the one and the zero. The one represents perfection and the zero represents its antithesis, everything and nothing. Dante helps us understand why number 10 represents bipolarity: he describes hell as it is formed by nine circles plus one forest, or a total of 10. Heaven represents nine spheres plus the Empyrean: again, 10. Heaven and Hell are the two opposites. Even the Pythagorean philosophers considered 10 to be the perfect number."

"We're missing one number, William. What could it be?"

"Let's see. Caracalla expresses anger by wrinkling his forehead, lowering his eyebrows and making them converge toward the center. Anger is the typical emotion felt during a fight. In ancient times, it was felt most frequently during battle. The last number of the code is definitely 12. According to mythology, Hercules, in a fit of rage, killed his family; in order to expiate his sins, he performed the famous 12 labors, one of which was catching Cerberus, the three-headed dog and guardian of the underworld. 12 is also the number of the Titans that fought angrily against the 12 Gods of Olympus. The Titans were defeated and locked up in Tartarus, a terribly dark place."

William pulled a pencil out of his pocket and wrote down the number sequence to release the power of the pinecone on a piece of paper: 3, 7, 10, 12.

He opened the case, taking care not to remove the pinecone from the niche where it was stored. There were five mobile dials that needed to be rotated to activate it.

Beatrice spoke up. "The numbers on the code indicate how many clicks each moving part of the pinecone has to make, right?

"Yes. However, there are five parts to rotate, and we only have four numbers. One is missing."

They spent more time examining the faces of the sculptures, but found no other useful elements. Since Virgil was getting bored and wanted to leave, they returned to the Bona Fide.

They felt deep sadness in their hearts because they had not been able to find all the numbers in the code.

7. Sees

Evening came and the wind rose up, blowing fiercely through the city. William walked to the meeting place, taking the artifact with him, as agreed on the phone with Valentino. He arrived at the bridge near Tiber Island, but although he was on time, no one was there waiting for him. The river flowed silently by, carrying along large, smooth pieces of wood that from time to time crashed into each other.

"How much this river has witnessed over the centuries," he thought to himself. As such thoughts flowed through his mind, a voice broke the silence.

"Mr. Pattern, we meet again."

William was taken aback. As had happened the previous time, Valentino seemed to appear out of nowhere.

"You startled me, Valentino."

"I'm sorry. Did you go looking for the codes to activate the pinecone? So, you actually believe in its power now?"

"I don't understand how you knew that… but the fact is that I still believe in science."

William handed the briefcase to Valentino, who quickly opened it; as soon as he saw the pinecone, a strange glow appeared in his eyes. Then he nodded in satisfaction. "I will take it to a safe place and will continue to guard it. I will keep it away from those who might misuse its power. Now I have three questions for you."

"Go ahead, Valentino."

"If I asked you to guard the pinecone, would you accept?"

"No, I would not accept," William replied, puzzled by the strange question.

"If I offered you the chance to use the power of the pinecone to give people back their emotions, would you accept?"

"No, I wouldn't accept. I would try to use science."

"If I offered you the chance to use the power of the pinecone so that you could become a rich and powerful person, would you accept?"

"I would not accept. I just want to go back to living in the country with my family and teaching at the university."

"Good, Mr. Pattern. Clearly my questions were aimed at whether you were worthy, like your father, of guarding the codes."

"I don't want to be the guardian of anything. Now I have a few questions for you. Are you a member of the Rosicrucians? Why was my father the keeper of the codes? Was he part of some secret order?"

As if he had not heard any of the questions that William had asked, Valentino said, "One cannot choose to be the keeper of the codes, much less to be part of our family. One is called to do so. If I am not mistaken, you are missing the last number of the code to activate the pinecone. Well, the symbol found on the bottom of the plate on the Elpis has to do with the second number of the code. You are an astute person. It won't take you long to figure out what the number is: just look in the right direction. Having said that, I officially appoint you the keeper of the codes. You should not reveal the number sequence, not even under torture, not even if it means losing your life."

"I gave you back the pinecone. I think I'm entitled to some answers now."

After pondering for a moment, Valentino sighed. "I cannot tell you much. For centuries we were forced to hide away; we were not part of the dominant side, but we used the strong powers we had to spread our message. Let me explain. Throughout the centuries we have hidden our symbols in works of art, such as paintings. You certainly know some of them because they are famous. We also hid them in literary works. Many poets went down in history as champions of these strong powers and their works were diffused all over the world. In fact, many literary figures were part of our family. Their texts were full of code phrases, numbers and symbols: they helped spread the word. Mr. Pattern, we don't like to live in the shadows, but we were forced into them in order to survive."

"At least tell me who these artists are."

"It is what it is," Valentino said with a perfect British accent and then repeated it in Spanish: "*Es lo que es.*"

"What do you mean *It is what it is?* I think I have the right..." William didn't even have time to finish the sentence when Valentino disappeared into the evening shadows. It was unbelievable: once again, this mysterious man seemed to have vanished into thin air.

Who were the powerful ones that Valentino mentioned? Which artists had hidden messages, numbers and symbols in their works? William had no idea. According to Valentino, the symbol found on the bottom of the plate on the Elpis would lead him to discover the second number of the code. He suggested looking in the "right direction" What did he mean?

"A circle with a triangle inside, which in turn enclosed a square and a smaller circle," William murmured. "Of course! The solution was right in front of me all along, how could I have not realized it before! The symbol found on the plate hides the numbers of the code that are identical to those found in the Capitoline Museums! Both the faces of the emperors and the symbol found in the plate express the same numerical sequence! The first number of the code we found in the museums was 3: there were three geometric figures present in the symbol found in the plate, or the triangle, the square and the circle. The second number we discovered by looking at the busts of the emperors was 7. In geometry the number seven is represented with a heptagon, composed of seven points arranged around the perimeter of a circle. In this case, too, the circle appears in the symbol found on the ship. Then, at the Capitoline Museums we also found the number 10, which is represented by Pythagoreans as an equilateral triangle; in this case, this geometric figure is found within the symbol. Finally, observing the busts of the emperors, we discovered the number 12, which also has to do with the symbol; by multiplying the number of the three geometric figures of circle, square and triangle by the four sides of the square, which is to say the 3 geometric figures x 4 sides of the square = 12. Valentino suggested that I look in the "right direction!" That's the direction! He was alluding to the four cardinal directions: so, the last number in the code is 4, which corresponds to the four sides of the square in the symbol which was found at the bottom of the plate. Valentino said that the missing number was the second one. So, the right numerical sequence to activate the pinecone is: 3, 4, 7, 10, 12."

Satisfied with having discovered the connection between the symbol found on the bottom of the plate and the busts in the Capitoline Museums, and with having obtained the complete sequence of the code to activate the pinecone, William returned to the Bona Fide. The streets of the city were deserted and windswept; the dusty signs gave the alley and narrow streets a ghostly appearance. The surface of the road was starting to become slippery as a few timid drops of rain started to fall, announcing the arrival of a storm. As soon as he reached the lobby, Beatrice came to him.

"William, your companions are waiting for you in the meeting room," she said, with visible concern on her face. "It's urgent."

"OK, Beatrice, thank you. I also have some news."

"Tell me! I'm curious. Did you find out what the last number in the code is?"

William realized that if he shared that secret with his wife, revealing the code to activate the pinecone, he would expose her to great danger, so he simply said, "No, I returned the pinecone to its rightful owner. I'll tell you later what he told me. Now let's go join the rest of the group."

Walking into the meeting room, he saw his companions from Emosemvi and members of the Elpis crew talking among themselves. As soon as they saw him, they all stood up. But, as usual, he gestured for them to sit down and do away with all formalities.

Romance was the first to speak. "Our spies intercepted a ship from Africa bound for the port of Contempt City and managed to recover part of its cargo." He pulled a pinecone-shaped object out of a bag and placed it on the table, illustrating its characteristics to all present. "This is a replica of the ancient pinecone artifact. It is filled with Em 0 in gaseous form. If inhaled, it enters the system quickly and causes emotions to be lost in a very brief amount of time. It is even more effective than its earlier version in liquid form. This is what Ross spoke of to William in the underground bunker."

"No good news?" asked William wryly.

"Unfortunately, no. If we don't blow up the production facility for these pinecones, the people at MC will continue to ship them around the world, regroup, and strike even harder."

William tried to come up with a plan but he was tired and unmotivated. Leading an assault in Africa would mean risking his life again. On the one hand, Emosemvi was founded by his father, and he felt obliged; on the other was his family. This time he was deeply conflicted. He had been through a lot and had no energy to face a new battle.

Bringlux broke the silence. "Perhaps I can help. I have many friends and some of them are scientists who are still able to feel emotions. Thanks to their valuable contribution we were able to create a new gaseous version of Reversing. It is so powerful that it does not require the person who inhales it to experience the seven basic emotions within an hour. We only need to start producing the Reversing in such a quantity that we can distribute it around the world."

William, his eyes hopeful, spoke up. "All right. We will leave for Africa and attack the Tartarus bunker to stop the production of Em 0. Then we will convert that plant and use it to produce the new Reversing. If MC has no leader and if they are in disarray, once we take out their last remaining active headquarters, we will have won the battle."

Everyone looked at each other and nodded, showing that they were happy that he had come up with a plan to defeat MC and restore order to the world. Beatrice took little Virgil in her arms.

"I'm sorry but not this time, William. Go ahead and plan the attack, but we can't let you go to Africa. Our family is together now, and we risked losing everything. You must leave it to others to complete this mission."

"Beatrice, you don't understand, we are one step away from victory..."

With tears in her eyes and her voice broken with emotion the woman interrupted him. "We made a promise, remember? Together, beyond the bounds of emotions." Sighing, she added, "William, a leader knows when to back down. You are a hero and everyone in this room knows that you are, everyone also knows that you are willing to sacrifice your own life for Emosemvi. Please, do this for our son, Virgil. I would like to give him a happy childhood and a normal life."

A long silence followed Beatrice's words. All eyes were on him, waiting to hear how he would reply to his wife.

Tobia placed a hand on William's shoulder. "Your wife is right, you can't spend your life fighting. Now is the time to stop and spend some time with your family. Your son will be grateful. When James and I were on the mission in Calicraston Ville music building, we discovered skeletons in a room at the top of a flight of stairs. One of them wore a uniform with a patch that said "Mike" on it. It's time to give your father a proper burial, as his son. This is your mission now."

Little Virgil had been silent up until then. Although he didn't understand what was going on, he took the opportunity to speak up. "Dad, maybe we could bring Grandfather a flower together. Do you want to?"

William ran a hand over his face, clearing his throat. "All right, I'll take a step back. I will help you come up with a plan tonight for the assault on the Tartarus bunker. Although I will not be there physically, I will accompany you with my heart. My family and I will return home tomorrow."

Everyone there nodded, even though deep sadness lingered in their hearts. Without the guidance of their leader, they felt like a ship with a failing engine during a storm. They were all accustomed to fighting in extreme situations, but only William was able to instill in them the necessary courage to break through their opponent's defenses.

During the night, a plan was devised to conquer the Tartarus bunker. William knew perfectly well that if he planned a frontal assault, in all probability his companions would have been killed, so he focused on using cunning. With Bringlux's help he had to find a way to produce as much Reversing as possible so that he could spread it to the police and the military. In so doing, they could at least count on their support. Using armored vehicles, artillery, and the air force, the bunker would fall.

The next day Beatrice noticed an unusual sadness in her husband's eyes. She understood how difficult it was for him to back down in such a delicate moment. The end game was about to be played; his Emosemvi comrades might even die. She knew William well, and that he would have preferred to die fighting than to pass away as an old man in a hospital bed. Now, however, it was time to live a normal life.

8. Squaring the Circle

Before leaving the hotel, William hugged his companions hoping to see them again soon. Old Tobia looked more tired than usual: age was advancing and his muscles ached. But even he would not step down from doing battle, even though he had the right to do so.

"I hope to see you again," said William, turning to Bringlux.

"I hope not! Every time you show up at my hotel, you bring trouble! I think this time it's the end of MC."

William shook his head and smiled softly. He walked with Beatrice and Virgil towards the exit of the hotel where Valerio was waiting for them with the car to take them to the airport.

After a long trip they arrived back at their country house; everything was exactly as they had left it. Little Virgil seemed so happy to spend time with his parents. He was excited to be back home, reunited with his toys. When he was held prisoner with his mother, he dreamed of this moment… and now he felt safe again.

The days went by, with no news from Emosemvi. The television news didn't mention anything either. William continued to carry a gun with him since MC had not been entirely defeated and because the risk of being ambushed was still high. About a month after their return home, life had gone back to its natural rhythms and the days flowed quickly by. Virgil was always happy to go for walks in the countryside with his father and help his mother in the kitchen.

One evening there was a knock at the door. William took out his gun and went to open it. Standing before him were all his Emosemvi comrades: thinner, weary, but all in good shape. After affectionately embracing them one by one, he made them sit down. Romance came in first. He switched the TV to a news channel where a reporter was commenting on recent events.

"The well-known pharmaceutical company, Minedal-e Corporation, which everyone thought had been wiped out, has instead been plotting a criminal plan in the shadows for the past few years. After having, once again, erased all human emotions with Em 0 gas, MC agents prepared to launch their final attack, which would have spread their gas to the remotest corners of the planet. However, once again, Emosemvi, led by William Pattern, put an end to the evil aims of the pharmaceutical company. Performing a surprise attack with the support of the army, Emosemvi conquered the last stronghold of the MC located in the Niger desert. Stay tuned as we bring you more updates shortly."

William turned off the television. "You did it!"

"We all did it!" Romance clarified.

"I didn't do a single thing. You were on the front line."

"In truth, as soon as the Reversing spread among the military, we got all the support we needed. At dawn, the attack was launched. There were not many men outside the bunker, and those few who were there did not put up much resistance. With the help of the army, we injected a soporific gas into the ventilation system. The bunker was like an anthill, teeming with MC agents, and guess what? McMillan was there, too. As soon as the gas took effect we entered the bunker by blowing the front door. The occupants were all taken to the local jail to await trial. Our engineers started working right away to convert the plant and, soon enough, the pinecone replicas were filled with Reversing gas. The Elpis was the first ship to carry a cargo of Reversing overseas."

That evening, the Emosemvi crew disbanded. The battle had been won and order was restored to earth, perhaps for the last time. After thanking his comrades, William invited them to celebrate the defeat of the MC by spending some time together. He was eager for them to teach things to little Virgil, who was always so curious to learn about the feats that the members of the Resistance accomplished: he was proud that his grandfather had founded their organization.

The Calicraston Ville music studio became a safe harbor. There was no more trace of MC agents: they were either in prison or scattered around the world. One day, William went there with his Emosemvi comrades to retrieve James's body and the remains of his father, with the intention of taking them to the poppy field near the Fear City hydropower plant and giving them a proper burial. This was also where Tim was buried, the Emosemvi member who had died years before at mission's end.

The remains of James and Virgil, the founder of Emosemvi, finally found some peace in the poppy field. If he had still been alive, Virgil would've been proud of his son, how he had won the war, and how he had defeated MC for good. This time the phoenix would no longer rise from the ashes.

Who knew what secrets Virgil had brought with him to the grave. Why had he been chosen to be the keeper of the codes to activate the ancient pinecone artifact? Was he part of some secret society? Why had Valentino said he knew him? William wanted to know more, but the truth was buried underground with his father.

The clouds, looking down on the people gathered in that field of poppies, grew curious and wanted to huddle together, forming a current of cold air. From their gathering came rain, the first drops timidly wetting the ground, then taking courage and pouring down vehemently, until they beat so hard they bent the petals of the poppies to the ground, dyeing it red and creating a soft blanket.

Days went by. Life seemed to return to normal. Virgil went to school, Beatrice went back to restoring antique furniture, and William resumed teaching at the university. One day, at home, he turned on his television set and was pleasantly surprised to see the impressive spectacle of rose petals falling through the oculus of the Pantheon. Every year after the Pentecost mass, thousands of rose petals were thrown down from the height of forty-three meters into the dome, to symbolize the descent of the Holy Spirit. This very ancient ceremony celebrated the end of the harvest, which over time had taken on religious significance.

As thousands of rose petals fell lightly over the faithful and onto the ground, William stared in disbelief at the television set. Among the crowd was a man in a yellow shirt and red tie. Looking closely, he recognized Valentino, but then, in a whirlwind of petals, he disappeared.

William felt the desire to learn more about the relationship between the ancient artifact of the pinecone, the Rosicrucian Order, this mysterious Valentino, and his father Virgil, but he held himself back. He didn't know if the pinecone was a nexus of great power: what really mattered was that he had returned it to its rightful owners and that it was in a safe place.

The evening shadows had already taken possession of the sky when William and Beatrice led little Virgil to his room to tuck him in bed.

"Daddy, can you tell me a story? Can you tell me my favorite story? I want to hear the one in Latin."

After tenderly stroking his son's head, he replied carefully. "Today I'm going to tell you a new story. This one is full of numbers: remember it well, because one day you might want to tell it to your children."

Then, in the silent countryside, the three of them embraced each other tenderly. With tears of joy running down their faces and their hearts full of hope for the future, that evening their love was so strong that even the stars in the sky were moved with emotion.

THE END

Author's note

This section clarifies the meaning of some plot details. It is recommended that you do not read this section until you have finished the novel.

While William is sleeping in his country house, his grandfather appears to him in a dream. In his hands he holds a miniature bronze she-wolf, the hinges from a door, and a seal with a rose imprinted on it. William has no idea what those objects are for and especially why his grandfather has them in his hands in that strange dream. The grandfather says: "Another gift from Aesacus" and then disappears, after which the window suddenly opens and hundreds of lily flowers pour into the room. Aesacus is a figure from Greek mythology[1] with the gift of predicting the future and interpreting dreams. The miniature bronze she-wolf refers to William's future trip to Rome. The she-wolf intent on suckling the twins Romulus and Remus is, in fact, the symbol of the city of Rome; a famous ancient bronze sculpture lies in the Capitoline Museums.

The hinges from a door allude to the Alchemical Door, also known as the Magic Door, which is located in Piazza Vittorio Emanuele II in Rome. As William explains in the novel, this door really does exist and was one of the

[1] Apollodoro, *Biblioteca*, G. Guidorizzi, J.G. Frazer, Biblioteca Adelphi, 1995.

entrances to the now demolished villa owned by Massimiliano Savelli Palombara, Marquis of Pietraforte, friend of Queen Christina of Sweden, with whom he shared a passion for alchemy. The Marquis was a member of the Rosicrucians and in the basement of his villa there was an alchemical laboratory, where he conducted his experiments.

The seal with a rose imprinted on it alludes to what William will discover about the Rosicrucian Order in the city of Rome.

The large ship on which William embarks to go to Europe refers to the Greek myth of Pandora's box; in fact, on its side it is painted with an earthenware vase and it is named Elpis. In mythology "Elpis" is the spirit of hope that lives, along with others, in the box that Zeus gives Pandora.

On the ship, William makes the acquaintance of Medea, a scheming woman. In Greek, the name Medea means precisely that: schemer. In Greek mythology, Medea is in love with Jason and helps him steal the golden fleece that is guarded by a <u>dragon</u>. Moreover, the mythological figure of Medea <u>kills her own brother, Apsirto</u>, before boarding the ship, Argo.

In the novel, Medea has a tattoo of a <u>dragon</u> on her right forearm and <u>kills her brother</u> in the mess hall of the ship Elpis.

Also aboard the Elpis, William meets the ship's doctor, Acli, whose parents are an herbalist and a doctor that specializes in toxicology (a science that studies, among other things, the symptoms due to the effects of poisons and their action). Medea steals a poison from the infirmary and uses it to kill Madeline, William's mother. In the course of the novel, Acli prepares, at William's request, a substance capable of creating a state of apparent death, as well as different types of poisons to be used, eventually, in emergency situations.

In Greek mythology, Acli is the divinity of poisons and darkness.

The Bona Fide Hotel has <u>thirty-four</u> red banners with forked ends that hang from the window sills. They are lit at night by spotlights that fill them with light, making them look like fiery tongues. In the wind, the banners flutter rapidly, producing a peculiar sound. This gave rise to the popular legend that they were the tongues of the damned from hell, eager to tell the world their sad story. The number of colored red banners refers to the last canto (<u>thirty-four</u>) of the Divine Comedy's Inferno.[2] In that canto, after having met Lucifer, Dante and Virgil leave Hell and manage to "see the stars again."

The owner of the Bona Fide Hotel is called Bringlux. This name can be translated as "Light Bringer." We leave it to the reader's imagination to figure out who the owner of the hotel really is. He sits at the reception desk that is decorated with four colors: red, white, yellow and black.

---

[2] Alighieri D., op. cit.

The room assigned to William at the Bona Fide hotel is number <u>one hundred</u> and is located on the <u>third floor</u>. The Divine Comedy consists of <u>one hundred</u> cantos[3] divided into <u>three</u> parts, called "canti."

William, after speaking with Valentino, discovers that the code to activate the pinecone is contained both in the symbol found in the plate on the ship Elpis, and in the facial expressions of the sculptures in the Capitoline Museums. Hidden in the table of contents of this novel is the numerical sequence to activate the ancient artifact of the pinecone, namely: 3, 4, 7, 10 and 12. In fact, some chapter titles are palindromes. A palindrome is represented by a word, phrase, or numerical sequence that remains unchanged whether read from left to right or right to left. The title of Part II Chapter **3** is "Never Odd or Even" (note how this word can be read in either direction). The title of Part II Chapter **4**, "Live Not on Evil," can also be read backwards, as well as the title of Part **III**: Borrow or Rob?, while the title of Part III Chapter **5** is "Top Spot" and, finally, the title of Part III Chapter **7** is "Sees". So we have the numerical sequence 3, 4, 3, then 5 and 7. Observe its digits: **3** is the first number of the code to activate the pinecone, while the second number is **4**, then adding these two numbers (3+4) together, we get **7**, which is the third number of the code. The next number of the code to activate the pinecone is **10** and this is the sum of the

[3] Alighieri D., *La Divina Commedia. Commento e parafrasi,* San Paolo Edizioni, 1998.

previous numbers of the chapters: 3+4+3. The last number to complete the code to activate the pinecone is **12**, the sum of the numbers corresponding to the paragraphs where palindromes **5** and **7** appear (5+7= 12).

There are many other symbolic elements and historical references within the text, purposely not mentioned in this section so the reader can discover them one by one.

About the Author

Emiliano Forino Procacci is a psychologist and expert in verbal and non-verbal communication and the coding/decoding of facial expressions. After earning two master's degrees, he continued his training in London and California.

He has invented an innovative method for personnel selection based on assessment techniques, reading facial micro expressions and interpreting body language.

Instagram: fpemiliano

Facebook: Emiliano Forino Procacci

www.unstatusluxury.com

Bibliography

Alighieri D., *La Divina Commedia. Commentary and paraphrase*, San Paolo Editions, 1998.

Apollodoro, *Library*, edited by G. Guidorizzi, J.G. Frazer, Adelphi Library, 1995.

Cancellieri F., *Dissertazioni epistolari di G. B. Visconti e Filippo Waquier de la Barthe sopra la statua del discobolo scoperto nella Villa Palombara, arricchite con note e con le bizzarre iscrizioni della Villa Palombara,* Antonio Fulgoni, Rome, 1806.

Christiane L., *Pythagoras and his influence on thought and art*, transl.it by P. Faccia, Akeios, 2008.

Hesiod, *Theogony*, Trad. E. Romagnoli, BUR, 1984.

Sermonti V., *L'Eneide di Virgilio*, BUR, 2008.

The trilogy

A WORLD WITHOUT EMOTIONS (2020)

William Pattern's story begins in a world where people are no longer able to feel emotions. William is willing to go beyond all bounds to find out the truth of why things are this way. A series of twists and unexpected events lead the protagonist to encounter with an odd Resistance organization, thus discovering the importance of emotions, facial micro-expressions, and body language.

In a world filled with people with expressionless faces and ice-cold hearts comes a series of extraordinary events and an incredible love story intertwined with an action-packed plot and puzzles for the reader to solve.

A WORLD WITHOUT EMOTIONS: EVOLUTION (2021)

The third volume in **A WORLD WITHOUT EMOTIONS** trilogy is slated for publication in 2021.